PASSIONS AWAKENED

Book One Of The Passions Shared Trilogy

A STAG/VIXEN SAGA

Wade Alan

Case ID: 1-15143475508

First Edition 2026

Printed in the United States of America

.

Dedication

To E, forever my Vixen.

Acknowledgement

Writing Aaron and Jean has been a bit like watching two people you care about walk into a luxury resort with a suitcase full of hopes, insecurities, and questionable decisions—and then cheering them on anyway. This book grew out of curiosity, courage, and the belief that long-term love can still surprise you, delight you, and occasionally make you mutter, "Oh no… they're really doing that?"

To my countless readers on Fetlife.com who picked up this story and thought, Yes, I want to see what happens when honesty gets bold, thank you. You're the reason these characters breathe. Your messages, your enthusiasm, and your willingness to explore the deeper layers of connection keep this world alive.

To the couples out there who have ever whispered, "We could try that," or "Maybe we should talk about this," you inspired more scenes than you know. Your bravery in choosing each other—again and again—makes romance worth writing.

And to anyone who has ever looked at their partner and realized the adventure isn't over, it's just getting interesting… this book is for you.

Special Thanks

To the early readers Thank you for your honesty, your laughter, and your "Wait, I need a minute to process this" messages. You helped shape the emotional backbone of this story.

To Kelly, Anna, Eileen, Moriah, and Dave, the friends who listened to me talk through plot twists, you endured conversations that began with, "Okay, but what if they tried this?" and ended with, "No, no, that's too much—wait, is it?" Your patience deserves a medal.

To the quiet supporters, the ones who said, "Keep going," when the draft was messy, the characters were stubborn, and the coffee was running low. You know who you are.

And finally, to Aaron and Jean, thank you for showing up in my imagination with all your flaws, fears, and fire. You made this journey worth taking

Table of Contents

Preface

What a "Stag/Vixen" Relationship Is

A **Stag/Vixen** relationship is a form of consensual non-monogamy in which:

- The **Stag** is (usually) the male partner who enjoys and supports his female partner having additional sexual partners.
- The **Vixen** is (usually) the female partner who explores those outside connections.
- The dynamic is typically **confident, collaborative, and non-humiliating**.
- The couple usually maintains a strong primary bond, emphasizing communication, trust, and mutual enthusiasm.

This arrangement is often framed as empowering for both partners:

- The Vixen has the freedom to explore.
- The Stag takes pleasure in her confidence, desirability, and autonomy.

It's a style of ethical non-monogamy rooted in mutual respect, not degradation. In this saga, the Stag (Aaron) is male, and the vixen (Jean) is female.

How It Differs from Cuckold Dynamics

While both involve one partner having outside partners, the tone and emotional structure are very different.

Key Differences

Aspect	Stag/Vixen	Cuckold
Emotional tone	Confidence, pride, shared excitement	Often includes themes of humiliation or submission (when consensual)
Role of the male partner	Active, supportive, sometimes participating	Often submissive or intentionally excluded
Power dynamics	Generally equal	Often includes power imbalance (again, consensual when healthy)
Motivation	Celebration of the Vixen's autonomy and desirability	Exploration of erotic humiliation, denial, or submission

A Stag is **not** seeking humiliation; he's seeking connection, erotic adventure, and shared experience.

How It Differs from BDSM Relationships

Stag/Vixen dynamics can overlap with BDSM, but they are not inherently BDSM-based.

- BDSM focuses on **power exchange**, roles (Dominant/submissive), and sometimes physical or psychological intensity.
- Stag/Vixen focuses on **sexual openness and shared enthusiasm**, not power play.

Some couples blend the two, but they are separate frameworks.

In Short

A **Stag/Vixen** relationship is a confident, collaborative form of consensual non-monogamy centered on:

- Mutual respect
- Clear communication
- Enthusiastic consent
- Shared erotic interest in the Vixen's outside experiences

It differs from cuckolding by avoiding humiliation themes, and it differs from BDSM by not requiring power exchange.

Prelude

My name is Aaron Thorne. My wife Jean and I have been together for twelve years. I founded a small data security company back when that industry was in its infancy. I have done well over the years, which gives us a certain freedom that most other couples are not able to enjoy. She is an amazing woman, as you will see!

I learned long ago that she had a certain set of talents that were just too amazing for me to keep to myself. We are monogamish, which means we generally don't sleep around. When we do have an urge to color outside the lines, we do it together. You see, Jean is a nymphomaniac. That's a fancy word for a woman who just can't seem to get enough sex. She cannot be satisfied. I also realized that I take great satisfaction in sharing her with others, and in watching the way she uses her skills to give great pleasure to both men and women.

We also love to live out our fantasies. Our lifestyle allows us that freedom. I mean, vanilla is nice, but there are zillions of other flavors, and sometimes we even add sprinkles!

Frequently, we play this little game where we sit together in a bar and just check out the other patrons as they come and go. If someone strikes our fancy, the seduction begins!

Most of the time, things go nowhere, but occasionally, when the stars and planets align, magic happens...

CHAPTER 1
Passions Genesis

"We've talked about this for months. Tonight, let's test the game!"

The words, a low murmur that cut through the din of the charity gala, weren't a threat. They were a promise. A delicious, shiver-inducing promise that Jean felt more than heard, spoken directly into the space between her shoulder blades as Aaron's hand settled on the small of her back. His touch was proprietary, warm through the emerald silk of her dress.

She didn't turn. Instead, she took a slow sip of her champagne, letting the bubbles dance on her tongue, and leaned back just a fraction into his solid presence. The room was a sea of black ties and glittering gowns, a fundraiser for the city's new tech incubator. Aaron's domain, and tonight, her playground.

"Is that a corporate objective, Mr. Thorne?" she asked, her voice a study in casual indifference as she watched a group of investors cluster around a holographic display. "Or a personal one?"

His fingers flexed against her spine, a subtle, possessive pressure. "The two have always been delightfully intertwined where you're concerned, Mrs. Thorne."

Mrs. Thorne. He used it like a secret code. In this room, it was a fact, a legal designation. Between them, it was a trigger, a reminder of the contract that went far beyond the marriage license. The one that allowed for nights like this. The game was on.

***

It had started that morning, over coffee and spreadsheets.

Aaron's home office was all clean lines and muted greys, a reflection of the man himself: controlled, efficient, formidable. At forty-five, he had the lean build of someone who viewed the corporate gym as a strategic battlefield and the sharp, assessing gaze of a man who built a data security empire from a dorm room idea. He was scrolling through a threat report, his brow furrowed.

Jean, at thirty-eight, padded in wearing one of his old, soft cotton t-shirts and nothing else. She placed a fresh mug next to his elbow, then leaned her hip against his desk, effectively blocking his view of the monitor.

"The Wallace Foundation Gala?" she asked, as if announcing the day's most critical agenda item.

He looked up, the tension in his shoulders easing as he took her in. The morning light caught the hints of copper in her otherwise dark hair, still sleep-tousled. His gaze traveled down, over the familiar drape of the fabric, and a faint, appreciative smile touched his lips. "The obligatory schmooze-fest. Black tie. You'll need a dress."

"I have a dress," she said, a slow smile spreading across her face. "The question is, what's the objective?"

Aaron leaned back in his chair, steepling his fingers. "Primary objective: secure a soft commitment from David Chen for the Series C funding. He's the keynote. Secondary objective: reinforce our brand as the stable, unshakeable bedrock of the industry. Tertiary..." He let the sentence hang, his eyes darkening as they met hers.

"Tertiary?" she prompted, her voice dropping to a murmur.

"Tertiary objective," he said, reaching out to hook a finger in the hem of the t-shirt, drawing her a step closer, "is field testing our new dynamic."

Jean's pulse gave a little kick. "Oh?"

"The room will be full of predators," he said, his thumb stroking the sensitive skin of her inner thigh. "Sharks who think because they can move a decimal point, they own the ocean. I want them to see what I have. I want them to *want* what I have. And I want them to understand, on a visceral level, that they can look, and maybe touch, but that you are *mine*, and your complete attention is a prize I alone can win."

A thrill, hot and sharp, shot through her. It wasn't about ownership in a crude sense. It was about an exhibition. About the electric current of being *seen* as his most prized, most secret asset. About the power she held in that role. The vixen to his stag.

"Public rules?" she asked, her breath catching slightly as his thumb moved higher.

"Flirtation is encouraged. Physical escalation... remains at my discretion." His voice was all business, but his eyes were lit with a familiar, predatory heat. "The goal is tension. Maximum tension. Let them see the chemistry. Let them wonder. Let them imagine possible outcomes."

He withdrew his hand, the loss of contact a sudden chill. "Now, go be devastating. My eleven o'clock is about to call in."

***

The dress was indeed devastating. A column of emerald green silk that clung to every curve before falling in a liquid pool at her ankles. The back was a plunge that stopped just shy of daring, held together by a single, delicate clasp. It was a dress that whispered, then laughed. She'd paired it with simple diamonds at her ears and a bare face save for a slash of red on her lips—a decision Aaron had approved with a silent, heated look that felt like a touch.

The drive to the museum where the gala was held was a study in contained energy. Aaron drove his sleek, silent electric car with focused precision, one hand on the wheel, the other resting on her bare knee. His touch was a brand.

"Chen is traditional. Respectful of hierarchy. He'll approach me first," Aaron said, outlining the playbook. "You'll be charming and intelligent; ask a question about data sovereignty in the Pacific Rim. He'll be impressed. He'll then try to engage you directly, to test my reaction."

"And your reaction?" Jean asked, tracing the line of his jaw with her eyes.

"My reaction will be to give you my full attention when he speaks to you," Aaron said, a sly grin touching his lips. "As if I'm hanging on your every word, too. It will unbalance him. He'll think he's won a point, stealing your focus. He won't realize I'm directing the entire exchange."

It was this chess-game mindset that thrilled her as much as the physical promise. Their relationship was a secure fortress, built on years of trust and a shared, hungry curiosity. The open arrangement—her adventures as the vixen, his composed watchfulness as the stag—wasn't a patch for something broken. It was an expansion pack for something already extraordinary. It allowed for moments like this, where the flirting was a performance with a single, rapt audience of one: each other.

***

The gala was in full swing when they arrived. Aaron was immediately absorbed into a vortex of handshakes and low, earnest conversation. Jean moved through the crowd like a separate, graceful current, accepting a glass of champagne, exchanging pleasantries with the wives of the other important guests, her smile never wavering. But her attention, like a homing beacon, was always pulled back to him.

She saw the moment David Chen, a trim man in his sixties with an air of quiet authority, approached Aaron. She watched Aaron's posture shift into "CEO Mode"—open, confident, slightly deferential without being weak. After a few minutes, as predicted, Chen's gaze slid to her, standing with a group a few feet away. Aaron followed his look, then smiled and gestured her over.

"David, this is my wife, Jean. Jean, David Chen of Aurelius Capital."

"A pleasure," Chen said, taking her hand. His grip was firm, his eyes keenly appreciative behind his glasses. "Aaron's been monopolizing you. I was just telling him his insights on zero-trust architecture are the most coherent I've heard."

"He has a way of cutting through the noise," Jean said, her smile warm. She let her hand linger in Chen's for a beat longer than strictly necessary before gently extracting it. "But I'm curious, David—how do you see that architecture holding up under the new ASEAN data localization proposals? Isn't the very concept of 'zero-trust' challenged by mandated geographic borders?"

Chen's eyebrows lifted. He glanced at Aaron, who was watching Jean with an expression of rapt, proud fascination, as if she'd just revealed a hidden talent for astrophysics.

"An excellent question," Chen said, turning fully to her. And just like that, the dynamic shifted. Aaron had ceded the floor, but he held the strings. Jean held Chen in a lively, technical debate for five minutes, her insights sharp, her laughter light. She could feel Aaron's gaze on her like a physical warmth. She could also feel the glances from other men in the group, their interest piqued.

When Chen was pulled away by an associate, he bowed slightly to her. "A true pleasure. Aaron, you're a lucky man. In more ways than one."

The moment he was out of earshot, Aaron's hand found the small of her back again. "Perfect," he murmured, his lips close to her ear. "You had him eating out of your hand. He'll remember you, not the proposal. That's the hook."

The evening unfolded as a series of such maneuvers. Jean would engage, dazzle, and retreat, always returning to Aaron's side, where his touch—a hand on her back, fingers brushing her arm, a palm settling possessively on her hip—would reassert the connection. The tension between them began to hum, a private frequency in the public noise.

During a slow, instrumental piece, they danced. Not close, not in this crowd, but with a precise, formal space between them. It made every point of contact electric: his hand on her waist, her hand on his shoulder.

"You're enjoying this," he stated, his voice low.

"Immensely," she breathed back, her eyes on his. "The woman in the silver gown by the orchid display hasn't taken her eyes off you all night. She thinks she's being subtle."

"I hadn't noticed," he said, and it was the truth. His entire world had narrowed to the woman in his arms, to the game they were playing. "What about the young hedge-fund idiot who's been refilling your champagne glass a little too eagerly?"

"He's harmless. All appetite, no strategy." She tilted her head, a vixen assessing prey. "Unlike you."

"My strategy is simple," he said, pulling her a fraction closer as they turned, the silk of her dress whispering against his tuxedo. "I let the asset appreciate in full view of the market. Let the bids rise in their imaginations. And then..." He guided her into a slow dip, his face hovering above hers for a heart-stopping moment. "...I execute a private buyback."

The heat in his eyes was almost unbearable. She could feel the promise in his words, a physical ache building low in her belly. The music ended. They didn't move for a second, trapped in the charged space between them.

As they left the dance floor, the air crackled. The teasing, the looks, the whispered promises—it had all been kindling. Now, she could feel the first real flames.

They were near the entrance to a shadowy hallway that led to the museum's private donor galleries, now closed for the evening. Aaron's hand was a firm guide on her back, steering her subtly away from the main crowd.

"Primary and secondary objectives are met," he murmured, his breath warm against her temple. "Chen is in. The brand is... reinforced."

"And the tertiary objective?" Jean asked, her voice barely a whisper.

He stopped at the mouth of the dim hallway. It was deserted, a pool of quiet darkness compared to the glittering ballroom. He turned her to face him, his hands settling on her hips. The noise of the gala was a muffled backdrop.

"Field testing," he said, his eyes roaming her face, drinking in the parted lips, the dilated pupils. "We've established the tension. Now we measure its breaking point."

He didn't kiss her. That would be too direct, too simple a release. Instead, he leaned in, his mouth hovering just beside hers. She could feel the heat of his skin, smell the clean, familiar scent of him mixed with faint cologne. His thumb stroked the dip of her waist, where the silk was thinnest.

"I can feel your heart racing," he whispered, his lips brushing the corner of her mouth with the ghost of a touch. "Right through the dress. Everyone out there sees a confident, beautiful woman. But I know. I know what this is doing to you."

He pulled back just enough to look into her eyes. The possessive intensity there stole her breath. "This is the part where they imagine what happens next. Where *you* imagine what happens next. Do you want to know what I'm imagining, Jean?"

She couldn't speak. She could only nod, a slight, desperate motion.

His voice dropped to a rough, velvet-soft growl, meant for her ears alone.

The darkness of the hallway felt like a sanctuary, the distant hum of the gala a world away. Aaron's question hung in the charged air between them, a promise wrapped in a threat, a delicious suspense that coiled tight in Jean's belly. She wanted to hear it. She needed to hear it.

But the sharp click of dress shoes on marble shattered the moment.

Aaron's head turned a fraction, his gaze slicing toward the sound. His hands didn't leave her hips, but his grip shifted from possessive to protective, then back to possessive again. A figure paused at the entrance to the hallway, silhouetted by the ballroom lights.

David Chen adjusted his glasses, a polite, apologetic smile on his face. "Aaron. Jean. Forgive the intrusion. I was just looking for the gentlemen's lounge. This museum is a maze."

The lie was smooth and practiced. He hadn't been looking for a restroom. He'd been looking for *them*. Jean felt the shift in Aaron instantly, the predatory heat banked behind a mask of polished civility. It was a transformation she'd seen a thousand times, but it never failed to thrill her. The man who'd just been whispering about the intimacy they would share was gone, replaced by the CEO.

"Just down that way to the left, David," Aaron said, his voice calm and friendly as he subtly shifted his body to block Jean from Chen's direct view. It wasn't obvious. Just a husband standing close to his wife. "Easy to miss."

"Thank you." Chen's eyes lingered on Jean for a heartbeat too long. There was appreciation there, intellectual and aesthetic, but beneath it, a flicker of something else. A curiosity about the dynamic he'd interrupted. "I hope I'm not disturbing a private moment."

"Not at all," Jean said, finding her voice. It came out steady, laced with just the right amount of warm amusement. "We were just debating the merits of early Renaissance art versus the modern installations. Aaron thinks Caravaggio is melodramatic."

Aaron's lips quirked. He played along effortlessly. "I said his use of chiaroscuro is heavy-handed. Jean disagrees. Violently."

Chen chuckled, the sound rich and genuine. "A debate for another time, perhaps. I should let you return to it. And to the party. The hedge fund cavalry has arrived, I see. Young Mr. Harrington from Apex Capital is holding court by the bar." His gaze settled on Aaron, keen and assessing. "Ambitious. Aggressive. A lot of appetite, as you might say. But his fund's liquidity is... noteworthy."

With a final, slight nod, Chen turned and walked back toward the light, his message delivered. He wasn't just pointing out a party guest. He was offering intelligence. A potential piece for their board.

As his footsteps faded, the tension in the hallway didn't dissipate; it changed shape. It became strategic and focused. Aaron turned back to Jean, but the raw hunger from moments before was now channeled, laser-guided.

"Chen can't be the play," Aaron murmured, his voice all business, though his thumb was tracing slow, distracting circles on her silk-clad hip. "Too valuable. Too connected. Bad for business to muddy those waters."

Jean understood. The venture capitalist world was a small, gossiping pond. A misstep with a kingmaker like Chen could ripple out for years. "He was testing the boundary," she said softly. "Seeing how close he could get."

"And he saw me pull you back," Aaron said, a flicker of satisfaction in his eyes. "He understands the layout of the territory now. That's useful." He glanced back toward the murmur of the gala.

"But the hedge fund guy… Harrington. He's been orbiting you all night. Refilling your glass. Laughing a little too loud at your jokes."

"All appetite, no strategy," Jean repeated her earlier assessment, but now it felt like a profile being readied for a mission.

"Exactly," Aaron said, a slow, wicked smile spreading across his face. It was the smile he got when a complex encryption algorithm finally cracked. "Appetite is predictable. It's exploitable. And his fund's liquidity is, as Chen so delicately put it, noteworthy." His hands slid up to her waist, pulling her firmly against him. The hard lines of his body were a shocking contrast to the soft silk. "So. Tertiary objective adjustment. The field test needs a new subject."

Her breath hitched. "What are the parameters?"

"You have my permission," he said, the words deliberate, loaded, "to take things as far as you would like with young Mr. Harrington. Flirtation. Engagement. Let him feel the heat. Let him think he has a chance." He leaned in, his lips brushing the shell of her ear, his voice dropping to that low, possessive growl that went straight to her core. "You know I love to watch."

A shudder of pure, undiluted arousal rocked through her. This was it. The game is elevated. Not just being seen as his, but performing the act of being *almost* someone else's, under his exacting gaze. The power of it was intoxicating.

"How far?" she whispered, needing the clarity, the contract solidified.

"Your discretion," he breathed, kissing the sensitive spot just below her ear. "Just remember the audience. And remember who you come home to." He pulled back, his eyes burning into hers. "The goal is the same. Maximum tension. For him. For you. For me. Let's see what that breaking point feels like, darling."

With a final, searing look, he released her. He straightened his cufflinks, the picture of composed elegance, then offered her his arm. "Shall we?"

They re-entered the gala not as a couple fleeing a heated moment but as a king and queen returning to survey their court. The air felt cooler, the lights brighter, every sense heightened. Jean's skin felt hyper-alive, humming where he'd touched her. She scanned the room and found him almost immediately.

Robert Harrington was maybe thirty, with the fit, restless build of a former college athlete and the expensive, slightly too trendy tuxedo of someone still trying to buy his way into the old-guard club. He stood near the bar, surrounded by a few younger associates, his laugh booming over the din. His eyes, however, kept wandering. Searching.

When they found Jean, they stopped. Locked. A spark of pure, undiluted interest flashed across his face.

Aaron saw it too. He squeezed her arm gently against his side. "Game on," he murmured, his tone light, conversational. "I'll be with Timmons from the Journal. I'll have a perfect view."

He let her go, melting into the crowd with a few parting words to a gray-haired man with a press badge. Jean was alone. Or rather, she was a solo vessel, carrying the weight of her husband's intense, hidden focus. She felt it like a physical touch between her shoulder blades.

She took a slow breath, letting the vixen surface. It wasn't an act, not really. It was a part of her that only this game, this trust, could set free. She glided toward the bar, the emerald silk whispering promises with every step.

Robert Harrington saw her coming. He excused himself from his group with a practiced ease and met her halfway. "Jean. I was hoping I'd get another chance to talk. You vanished."

"Just a bit of fresh air," she said, smiling up at him. She let her eyes linger on his for a beat, then glanced down at his empty glass. "You're in need of a refill. As am I."

He signaled the bartender with a quick finger. "Champagne for the lady. And a Macallan 18, neat, for me." He turned his full attention to her. "So, 'fresh air.' Sounded pretty intense back there with your husband. Everything okay?"

The question was bold and probing. Testing the waters. Jean took the flute from the bartender, her fingers brushing Robert's deliberately in the transfer. A tiny, electric contact.

"Everything is perfect," she said, her voice a warm, intimate murmur. "Aaron is just... very passionate about his opinions. And about me." She took a sip, watching him over the rim of the glass. "It can be a lot sometimes."

She let the implication hang, a delicate, ambiguous offering. *I am cherished, maybe a little too tightly.*

Robert's eyes darkened. He took a slow sip of his whiskey, his gaze never leaving hers. "A man would be a fool not to be passionate about you, Jean. The way you handled Chen earlier... that was a masterclass. Most of the women here are just arm candy. You're a secret weapon."

"I have my interests," she said, shifting slightly so the light caught the copper in her hair. She was hyper-aware of Aaron's location across the room. He was deep in conversation, but his posture was angled toward her. Watching. "Data, art, disruptive ideas. I get bored easily."

"I have nothing *but* disruptive ideas," Robert said, leaning in. He smelled of citrus cologne and expensive Scotch. "My fund specializes in shaking up stagnant sectors. It requires... a certain appetite for risk." His eyes dropped to her lips, then back up. "For excitement."

The dance was accelerating. Jean let her shoulder lean gently against his arm as someone jostled past. "Risk is only exciting when you know you can handle the consequences," she said softly. "Don't you think?"

"I always handle the consequences," he replied, his voice dropping to match hers. The space between them was shrinking, charged with a blatant, hungry energy. "And the rewards are usually worth it."

His hand came up, not touching her but hovering near the small of her back, an almost-touch that was more intimate than a grip. He was moving fast, just as Aaron predicted. All appetite. Jean felt a flush spread across her chest, a real one. The thrill of the play, the tangible heat of this handsome, eager man, and the searing knowledge of Aaron's gaze—it was a potent cocktail.

"Tell me one," she challenged, her eyes wide, inviting. "One disruptive idea."

He did. He launched into a spiel about leveraging blockchain for micro-insurance in emerging markets. It was smart, if a bit rehearsed. Jean listened, nodding, asking sharp questions that made his eyes light up. She laughed at his jokes, touching his arm briefly to emphasize a point. Each touch was a spark. She could see his confidence growing, his chest puffing slightly. He thought he was winning.

And all the while, she was burning up for Aaron. Every laugh she gave Robert was a silent message to her husband. *See? See what I can do?* Every flick of her hair was a performance for her audience of one. The arousal was a live wire inside her, strung tight between the two men.

"You're incredible," Robert breathed, his speech done. He'd moved closer. His whiskey-laden breath was warm on her cheek. "Most people's eyes glaze over when I talk about tokenization."

"I'm not most people," Jean whispered.

His control snapped. The almost-touch became real. His hand settled on her waist, low, his fingers splaying over the silk. It was a bold, claiming move. The heat of his palm seared through the thin fabric. Jean's heart hammered against her ribs. This was escalation. This was the line, wavering in the sand.

She didn't pull away. She let her body sway into the touch, just a fraction. She looked up at him through her lashes, her red lips parted. "Robert..."

"There's a balcony," he said, his voice rough. "Around the corner. It's quiet. We could talk more. Without the noise." His meaning was unmistakable.

This was it. The offer. The point where the field test could go from observation to... participation. Her discretion. Her choice. The tension was a physical ache, a throbbing need between her legs. She could go. She could let this hungry, handsome man lead her into the shadows and see how far the heat would take them. Aaron would watch. He'd see it all.

The thought made her dizzy.

She was about to answer, to let the "yes" or "no" form on her tongue, when she felt it. A shift in the atmosphere. A presence.

She turned her head, just slightly.

Aaron was no longer talking to the journalist. He was standing alone, near a towering floral arrangement. A fresh glass of champagne in his hand. His gaze was locked on them. On Robert's hand on her waist. His expression was unreadable from this distance—calm, observing. But his posture was a study in contained power. A stag, watching a rival approach his vixen.

He didn't move. He didn't scowl. He simply raised his glass, a tiny, almost imperceptible toast, to her. To *them*.

And in that moment, Jean knew the answer. The breaking point wasn't about how far she could go with Robert. It was about how intensely she could want Aaron *while* playing with Robert. The power wasn't in the act with another; it was in the magnetic pull back to her husband.

She turned back to Robert, her smile turning soft, regretful. She placed her hand over his on her waist, not pushing it away, but holding it. A gentle, definitive pause.

"The balcony sounds... perfect," she breathed, seeing the triumph flare in his eyes. "But not yet. The anticipation is the best part, isn't it?" She slowly, deliberately, lifted his hand from her waist and gave it a light, playful squeeze before letting it go. "Find me later. After the silent auction."

She pulled away then, leaving him standing there, stunned and heated. She didn't look back at him. She walked, her hips swaying just so, on a direct path across the crowded floor toward Aaron.

His eyes tracked her every step. As she neared, she saw the fire in them, banked but blazing. The possessive pride. The sheer, unadulterated hunger.

She stopped inches from him. The noise of the gala faded to a buzz. The world was just this man, this electricity.

"Well?" she whispered, her voice trembling slightly with the force of her own need. "Did I pass the test?"

Aaron's free hand came up and cupped her jaw, his thumb stroking over her cheekbone. The touch was devastating in its tenderness, a shocking contrast to the game they were playing. "You," he said, his voice a low, rough vibration she felt in her bones, "are exceeding every specification."

He leaned down, his lips a breath from hers. Not kissing. Just sharing air. Sharing the same charged, desperate space. "He touched you," Aaron murmured. It wasn't a question. It was a dark, thrilling acknowledgment.

"You said I could."

"I know." His thumb traced her lower lip. "I saw. And now," he said, his other hand finding the delicate clasp at the back of her dress, his fingers resting against it, "I believe it's time for the private buyback."

The clasp was a tiny, intricate thing. A single point of failure holding her entire world of emerald silk together. His fingers rested on it, not undoing it, but *claiming* it. The promise was so explicit, so public in its intimacy, that Jean's knees nearly buckled. Anyone could turn and see them like this, see his hand on the zipper to her dress, and see the raw, consuming focus in his eyes.

"Here?" she gasped, the word barely audible.

CHAPTER 2

Discovery on the Balcony

The heat from Aaron's fingers on the delicate clasp was a brand. The world narrowed to that single point of pressure at the base of her spine, the promise implicit in his touch. *Here?* The word hung between them, a breathless challenge.

His thumb stroked the sensitive skin just above the metal. "Not here," he murmured, his voice a dark caress that contradicted the possessive claim of his hand. "But soon. The anticipation is part of the buyback." He released the clasp but let his palm flatten against the small of her back, a searing imprint through the silk. "You have a move to make. Don't keep your audience waiting."

He was giving her the nudge. The final push into the deeper game. The look in his eyes was pure, unadulterated hunger—for her, for the spectacle, for the control. Jean felt a fresh wave of liquid heat pulse between her legs. She nodded, a quick, sharp motion, and took a half-step back. The loss of his touch was a physical ache.

"I need to freshen up," she said, her voice miraculously steady. "The champagne..."

"Of course." Aaron's smile was a wolf's smile. He lifted his own glass to his lips, his eyes never leaving hers as he drank. A silent toast. *Go on.*

She turned, feeling the weight of his gaze like a handprint on her body. She walked toward the restrooms, her steps measured, each one a conscious effort to keep her hips from swaying too much, too soon. The corridor to the ladies' lounge was quieter, lined with modern art that blurred in her peripheral vision. Inside, the cool, marble-lined space was empty. She braced her hands on the edge of a vanity, staring at her reflection. Her cheeks were flushed, her eyes brilliantly dark. The red of her lips was a stark, wanton contrast to her pallor.

He's watching. He's always watching. The thought wasn't a constraint; it was a catalyst. It stoked the fire. She ran a finger under her lower lip, blotting a nonexistent smudge, then reapplied her lipstick with a precise, deliberate stroke. Each motion was a ritual, a preparation for a sacrifice she was eager to make. She smoothed her hands over the emerald silk, feeling the way it clung to her dampening skin. A final, deep breath, and she turned.

Back in the ballroom, she didn't immediately seek out Robert. She let her gaze sweep the room, a queen surveying her territory. She found Aaron first. He had moved. He was now standing near the arched entrance to a balcony that overlooked the museum's sculpture garden, partially obscured by a large, leafy potted palm. A perfect vantage point. Shadowed, private, yet with a clear sightline to the balcony doors. He held a fresh glass of whiskey, his posture relaxed, but his attention was a laser sight trained on the space where she stood.

Their eyes met across the crowded room. He gave a single, almost imperceptible nod.

Game on for real.

Jean's heart hammered against her ribs. She turned, her scan of the room landing on Robert Harrington. He was still by the bar, but he'd been watching for her return. His eyes lit up the moment he saw her. She offered him a small, private smile—just a slight curve of her lips, a knowing tilt of her head—and then, without breaking the connection, she turned and began walking, not toward him, but toward the balcony doors.

It was an unmistakable invitation. A command, even.

She heard the quick shuffle of his steps behind her almost immediately. She didn't look back. She pushed through the heavy glass door, stepping out into the cool night air. The balcony was long and narrow, lit by soft, recessed lighting that left pockets of deep shadow.

The murmur of the gala became a distant, muffled hum. The only sounds were the faint rustle of leaves from the garden below and the rapid beat of her own heart.

The door clicked shut behind her.

She walked to the railing, placing her hands on the cool stone, and looked out over the dark shapes of sculptures. She felt him approach, felt the space around her grow warmer and charged.

"You came," Robert said, his voice tight with anticipation. He stood close beside her, not touching yet.

"You asked me to," Jean replied, still looking forward. She let the silence stretch, let the tension coil. Then she turned to face him, leaning back against the railing. The city lights glinted in her eyes. "It's quieter out here."

"Much." He moved in, his body caging her against the stone balustrade. The citrus and Scotch scent of him enveloped her. His hands came up to rest on the railing on either side of her hips, not touching her, but trapping her. "No more distractions."

She looked up at him, her expression open, inviting. "Just us."

That was all the permission he needed. His control, tenuous at best, snapped. One hand left the railing and cupped her jaw, his fingers sliding into her hair. His kiss was not a question. It was a demand. Hot, hungry, and slick with whiskey. His mouth slanted over hers, his tongue pushing past her lips without preamble.

Jean met the kiss with a moan that was only half-performed. The reality of it—the firm pressure of his mouth, the aggressive sweep of his tongue, the sheer *physicality* of a man other than Aaron—sent a jolt through her system. She kissed him back, letting her hands come up to rest on his chest, feeling the hard planes of muscle beneath the fine wool of his tuxedo. She could feel his heart pounding, a frantic rhythm against her palms.

Aaron is watching this. He's seeing his wife be kissed like this. The thought was a lightning strike of arousal. She arched into Robert, a silent encouragement.

He groaned into her mouth, his other hand finally leaving the railing to settle on her hip, his fingers digging into the silk. "God, you're incredible," he breathed against her lips before diving back in. His kiss grew messier, more desperate. His hand on her hip slid around to the small of her back, pulling her flush against him. She could feel the hard, insistent ridge of his erection pressing against her lower belly.

The sensation was a shock—a blunt, thrilling reality. She gasped into his mouth, and he took it as a sign of surrender. His kisses trailed down her jaw to the sensitive column of her throat. "I've wanted this all night," he muttered, his teeth scraping lightly over her pulse point. "Since I first saw you."

His hand on her back slid lower, cupping the curve of her ass through the silk, squeezing possessively. Jean's breath hitched. This was moving fast, just as she'd known it would. Just as Aaron had wanted it to. She let her head fall back, giving him better access to her throat, a silent offering. Her eyes, however, fluttered open. Over Robert's shoulder, through the glass door, she could see the vague, shadowed shape of a man standing by the potted palm. Watching.

See, she thought, the word a prayer and a taunt. *See what he wants. See what's yours.*

The dual awareness was intoxicating. Robert's mouth was hot and demanding on her skin, his hands rough and eager. And Aaron's gaze was a physical weight, a phantom touch that stoked every sensation to a higher flame.

Robert's hand left her ass and slid around to her front, his fingers skimming the side of her breast through the silk. "This dress," he groaned. "It's been driving me out of my mind." His palm closed over her breast, his thumb finding her nipple and rubbing it into a hard, aching peak through the fabric.

A sharp, genuine cry escaped her. The friction was exquisite, the slight roughness of his thumb pad a delicious contrast to the smooth silk. She pushed her chest into his hand, a wordless plea for more. He complied, kneading her breast, his mouth returning to hers in a ravishing kiss.

His other hand joined the fray, sliding down from her hip to the hem of her dress. His fingers crept underneath, finding the bare skin of her thigh. The touch was electric. His hand was warm and slightly calloused, and it slid upward with a single-minded purpose.

Jean's mind fragmented. Part of her was here, on this balcony, with this handsome, hungry stranger whose touch was sparking real, visceral pleasure. Her skin pebbled under his palm. Her core clenched, empty and aching. Another part of her was back in the ballroom, locked in Aaron's predatory gaze, performing for him, *belonging* to him in the most profound way possible precisely because she was here.

Robert's fingers reached the apex of her thighs. He stilled, his breath coming in ragged pants against her neck. "Tell me you want this," he demanded, his voice guttural.

She didn't have to fake the desperation in her whisper. "Yes."

His fingers slid beneath the lace edge of her thong. He made a raw, animal sound as he found her. "Fuck. You're so wet."

The first touch of his fingers to her bare, slick flesh was a revelation. A bolt of pure, carnal pleasure shot up her spine. He wasn't gentle. He circled her clit with a firm, insistent pressure, his touch confident, practiced. Jean's knees buckled. She grabbed onto the lapels of his tuxedo jacket for support, a low, continuous moan torn from her throat.

"That's it," Robert growled, watching her face as he worked her with his hand. His other arm wrapped around her waist, holding her up. "Let me hear you. You have no idea how badly I've wanted to hear you."

He plunged a finger inside her, then another, his palm grinding against her clit. The stretch, the sudden, shocking fullness, the relentless rhythm—it was overwhelming. Her hips began to move of their own accord, riding his hand, chasing the coil of pleasure tightening deep in her belly. Her moans grew louder, unchecked. The cool night air did nothing to cool the fire he was stoking.

"You're so fucking tight," he breathed, his own arousal evident in the strained pitch of his voice. He bent his head, his mouth latching onto her breast through the silk, sucking the hard nipple into the damp fabric. The dual sensation—the rough, wet pull on her nipple and the deep, driving penetration of his fingers—tipped her dangerously close to the edge.

Her eyes flew open again, seeking the shadow in the doorway. *Aaron. Are you seeing this? Are you seeing how wet I am for this game, for you?* The thought of his eyes on her, watching another man's fingers disappear inside her, watching her body arch and beg for it, was the final catalyst.

The orgasm ripped through her with shocking force. It wasn't the slow, deep unraveling Aaron could coax from her over hours. This was a sharp, brutal climax, a lightning strike of pleasure that seized her muscles and tore a ragged scream from her throat. She convulsed against Robert, her inner walls fluttering wildly around his thrusting fingers, her vision whiting out at the edges.

Robert held her through it, his fingers still working her, prolonging the waves until they subsided into trembling aftershocks.

She sagged against him, boneless, her breath coming in harsh, sobbing gasps. He slowly withdrew his hand, bringing his glistening fingers to his mouth and sucking them clean, his eyes locked on hers with primal satisfaction.

"You taste even better than I imagined," he said, his voice thick.

Jean was still reeling, her body humming, her mind a blissful stasis. But the game wasn't over. The most important audience member was still watching. She pushed weakly at Robert's chest, and he eased back, a triumphant gleam in his eye.

"My turn," he said, his hands going to his belt. The click of the buckle was loud in the quiet night. Jean reached for Robert's crotch, her fingers brushing against the hardness straining against his trousers. Her touch was deliberate and calculated, and Robert sucked in a sharp breath, his eyes widening as she unzipped his pants and reached inside. The heat of him seared her palm as she freed his cock, thick and throbbing in her hand.

She sank to her knees, the cool stone biting into her skin, but she barely noticed. Her eyes flicked up to meet his, holding his gaze as she wrapped her lips around him. His taste—musky, primal—flooded her senses as she took him deep into her mouth. Her left hand worked him, stroking in rhythm with her tongue, and the glint of her wedding ring caught the dim light, a stark reminder of the man watching from the shadows.

Robert's fingers tangled in her hair, his hips jerking forward instinctively as he groaned, a guttural sound that vibrated through her. "Fuck," he rasped, his voice unsteady. "You're flawless."

Jean didn't respond. She couldn't. Her focus was on the man above her, on the throbbing cock filling her mouth, and on the knowledge that Aaron was watching, his gaze a phantom touch that set her veins on fire. She sucked him greedily, her tongue swirling around the head, her throat opening to take him deeper. Her wedding ring glimmered with each stroke, a silent proclamation of whose game this truly was.

Robert's control unraveled with each passing second. His thighs trembled, his grip on her hair tightened, and his moans grew ragged, desperate. "Jean," he growled, his voice breaking. "I'm gonna"

She didn't let him finish. She took him deeper, swallowing every inch of him as he came with a shout, his release flooding her throat in hot, pulsing waves. She swallowed it all, her throat working greedily until he was spent, his cock still twitching between her lips.

When she finally pulled away, her lips swollen and glistening, she looked up at Robert, his face a mask of awe and disbelief. But her gaze flicked past him, to the shadowy figure beyond the glass door.

Aaron.

Her husband stood there, his expression unreadable, but his storm-dark eyes held hers with an intensity that made her shiver. She rose to her feet, her knees trembling, and wiped her mouth with the back of her hand, her ring catching the light once more.

Robert fumbled with his belt, his breaths still uneven, but Jean wasn't looking at him anymore. Her focus was on Aaron, on the silent promise in his gaze.

The game was theirs.

But before he could undo it, the balcony door swung open.

Aaron stood there, silhouetted by the light from the ballroom. He wasn't smiling. His face was an impassive mask, but his eyes burned with a dark, possessive fire that seemed to suck the warmth from the air. He held two glasses of champagne.

Robert froze, his hands still on his belt, a flush of anger and embarrassment rising on his neck. "Thorne. This is a private conversation."

"It looked very engaging," Aaron said, his voice calm and conversational as he stepped fully onto the balcony. He didn't look at Robert. His gaze was fixed on Jean, taking in her flushed face, her swollen lips, and the rapid rise and fall of her chest against the now-damp silk over her breasts. He saw everything. "But I'm afraid I must steal my wife back. A matter has come up that requires her... unique insight."

He extended one of the champagne flutes toward Jean. The gesture was absurdly normal, chillingly polite amidst the sexual havoc. "Darling?"

Jean's legs felt like water, but she pushed herself away from the railing. She avoided Robert's stunned, furious gaze and walked on unsteady feet toward her husband. She took the glass, her fingers brushing his. His skin was hot. A current passed between them, hotter than anything she'd felt with Robert.

"Of course," she said, her voice hoarse.

Aaron finally looked at Robert. His smile was thin, polite, and utterly devoid of warmth. "Harrington. Enjoy the rest of the gala. I'm sure we'll be in touch about those liquidity figures." He placed a guiding hand on the small of Jean's back—on the exact spot where the clasp had been, where Robert's hand had just been—and turned her, leading her back toward the light and noise.

As the door closed behind them, sealing Robert in frustrated silence on the balcony, Aaron leaned close, his lips grazing her ear. His voice was a low, vicious, thrilling rasp. "Delicious!"

CHAPTER 3

Discovery Poolside

A few days later, when the paperwork was complete and the deals were put in motion, Aaron booked a suite in a luxury resort so they could get away and celebrate. The heat of the encounter with Robert had subsided, but the thrill of the event lingered. They both knew that the game would continue!

The afternoon sun painted the infinity pool in molten gold, but Aaron's eyes weren't on the view. They were fixed on the curve of his wife's back, the way her simple black bikini clung to her skin as she leaned over the water's edge, talking animatedly with a man whose smile was too wide, too practiced.

Jean's laugh floated across the heated deck, a sound that usually made Aaron's chest swell with pride. Today, it made something else stir, low and possessive.

"See that?" Aaron murmured, not to Jean, but to the man seated next to him at the poolside bar. Cory was a new acquaintance, a finance guy from their corporate retreat wing of the resort, with a sharp gaze and an appreciation for fine things. Aaron had pointed him toward Jean an hour ago with a casual, *"My wife. Jean. She's something, isn't she?"*

Cory sipped his gin, his eyes following the same path Aaron's had. "I see it. She's got a spark. Not just the looks—the *energy*. You can feel it from here."

"You can," Aaron agreed, the pride genuine, layered with a darker, sweeter thrill. "Watch how she listens. Total focus. Makes a person feel like they're the only one in the world." He took a slow drink of his own bourbon, a Weller Antique, and the ice clinked softly. "It's a gift she has. Makes everyone want to be near her."

Across the pool, Jean finished her conversation, giving the man a friendly wave before turning. Her eyes found Aaron, and the spark Cory had noted seemed to intensify, directed solely at her husband. She started walking toward them, the water droplets on her skin catching the light, her stride confident and unhurried.

Cory leaned in slightly. "She's coming over."

"Of course she is," Aaron said, a smile playing on his lips. "She knows I'm watching."

Jean reached them, the scent of coconut sunscreen and chlorine mixing with her own warmer fragrance. She didn't sit; she stood beside Aaron, her hand resting lightly on his shoulder. Her touch was casual, but it sent a pulse of heat through his shirt.

"Making friends, darling?" she asked, her voice low and amused.

"Just sharing the view," Aaron replied, his gaze lifting to meet hers. There was a knowing glint in her eyes, a silent acknowledgment of the game. He turned back to Cory. "Jean, this is Cory. Cory, my wife."

"A pleasure," Cory said, standing briefly out of courtesy. His eyes lingered on Jean's face, then dipped, just for a fraction of a second, to the swell of her breasts against the bikini top. "Aaron's been telling me about your... spark."

Jean's smile deepened, a little crooked, a little wicked. "Has he? He's generous with his compliments." She squeezed Aaron's shoulder. "Sometimes too generous."

"Never too generous," Aaron countered, his voice firm. "It's all true." He let his hand drift up, catching hers on his shoulder, intertwining their fingers. The gesture was possessive, a public claim, and he felt her fingers tighten in response. *She liked it.*

"Well," Jean said, turning her attention back to Cory, though her body remained angled toward Aaron. "We're heading to the sunset lounge for cocktails soon. You should join us. The views are incredible."

Cory's expression brightened. "I'd like that."

CHAPTER 4

Discovery at the hotel bar

"You want me to suck your fucking cock right here, don't you?" Jean's voice was a low, husky promise in the damp night air.

The stranger, Tim, just grinned, his hands already on her hips. "I thought you'd never ask."

I leaned against our rental car, my own cock straining against my jeans, and watched.

But let me back up. It started an hour ago in the lobby bar.

We were on a weekend getaway, just the two of us. A chance to reconnect, to play. The hotel was nice, with all soft lighting and polished wood. We were sipping whiskey. I was tracing circles on Jean's knee under the table. She was wearing that green dress, the one that hugged her curvy frame, the neckline offering a generous view of her tits. I saw her eyes drift past me. I followed her gaze.

A man in a rumpled suit walked in. Late thirties, maybe forty. A salesman's confident weariness. He took the stool away from Jean. *Tim*, the bartender, called him.

Their eyes met. It wasn't an accident. Jean held his gaze for a beat too long, a slow smile playing on her lips before she looked down at her drink. I felt a familiar jolt of heat in my gut. *Showtime.*

I nudged her foot with mine under the bar. "See something you like?"

She bit her lip, her eyes sparkling. "He's got... a presence."

"Pushy," I murmured, watching Tim order a bourbon, neat, his voice too loud for the quiet room.

"I know," Jean said, and the way she said it, all breathy and knowing, made my heart pound. This was our game. Our delicious, filthy game. The stag. The vixen. And the lucky stranger.

The conversation was a formality. Tim introduced himself, his eyes glued to Jean's cleavage. He was in town for a conference. Bored. Lonely. His wedding ring was absent. Jean played along, laughing at his lame jokes, leaning in so he could smell her perfume. I stayed quiet, a silent partner in the conspiracy, my hand now openly on Jean's thigh, squeezing possessively, encouragingly.

It was maybe twenty minutes before Tim made his move. "This bar is dead. I've got a bottle of decent stuff in my car. Parked just out back."

Jean didn't look at me for permission. She looked at Tim. "Just a drink?" she asked, but the implication was anything but.

"Whatever you want it to be," Tim said, his voice dropping.

That's how we ended up in the shadowy corner of the parking garage, the hum of ventilation fans our only soundtrack. The air was cool and smelled of oil and concrete.

Now, Jean was pressed between Tim's body and the side of a black SUV. I had a perfect view.

"Go on, baby," I said, my voice rough. "Show him."

Jean's hands went to Tim's belt. He was already hard, a thick bulge tenting his dress pants. She made quick work of the buckle, the button, and the zipper. She didn't pull his pants down; she just yanked them open and reached in.

Her eyes went wide. "*Fuck*, Aaron," she breathed, her head tilting back to look at him over her shoulder. "He's so fucking thick."

"Let me see," I growled.

She pulled his cock out. And she was right. It was a beast. Thick, veiny, uncut, and already leaking at the tip. It jutted out from his groin, pale against the dark fabric of his pants. *My god.*

Tim groaned, his head thudding back against the SUV. "You're a fucking dream."

Jean didn't wait. She dropped to her knees on the concrete, the rough surface probably biting into her skin, but she didn't seem to care. She was in her element. An exhibitionist in her natural habitat, with her favorite audience watching.

She took him in her hand first, stroking the length, her thumb smearing the bead of pre-cum over the swollen head. "You like being watched, Tim? You like knowing my man is seeing every inch of his girl's lips wrapped around your big fucking cock?"

"Yes," he hissed, his fingers tangling in her curly hair.

"Tell me," I commanded, my hand rubbing my own hardness through my jeans.

"He loves it," Jean said, her eyes locked on Tim's. "He loves watching me be a fucking slut for a stranger's cock." Then she leaned forward and licked a long, slow stripe from the base to the tip.

Tim shuddered.

She opened her mouth and took just the head inside, her lips stretching into a perfect 'O.'. She swirled her tongue around the sensitive ridge, her eyes closed in concentration, in pure fucking bliss. A low moan vibrated from her throat around his flesh.

"That's it," I whispered, moving closer. "Take it deeper."

Jean obeyed. She began to bob her head, slowly at first, getting used to his girth. Her saliva glistened in the dim light. The sounds were obscene, wet, slurping, and perfect. *Suck. Slurp. Gag.*

She pulled off, gasping. "He's so big. He's fucking stretching my throat." She looked up at Tim, her lips slick and swollen. "You want to fuck my face, salesman? You want to use my fucking mouth?"

In answer, Tim's hands tightened in her hair. He didn't push, not yet. He guided. He pulled her back onto him, feeding her another inch, then another. Jean gagged, her body tensing, but she relaxed her jaw, letting him slide deeper. Tears welled in the corners of her eyes.

The sight was the most erotic thing I had ever seen. My Jean, on her knees, her pretty mouth stuffed full of another man's thick cock. Her mascara was starting to run. Her tits were spilling from the top of her dress, pushed up by her own arm as she braced herself against his thigh.

"Look at me, Jean," I said.

Her tear-filled eyes found mine. She held my gaze as Tim started to move, pulling his hips back and then sliding his cock back into her waiting, wet mouth. *In. Out.* A rhythm building. Her cheeks hollowed as she sucked with desperate, hungry pulls.

"You look so beautiful like this," I told her, my voice thick. "Such a good fucking slut for us."

She moaned around his shaft, the vibration making Tim curse. His thrusts became more urgent, less controlled. He was fucking her mouth in earnest now, the SUV rocking slightly with his force. Jean took it, her hands on his ass, pulling him deeper into her throat with every thrust.

"I'm going to come," Tim grunted, his voice strained. "I'm going to fill that pretty fucking mouth."

Jean's eyes flew open, wide and pleading on mine. A question. *My permission.*

"Do it," I said, the words leaving me in a rush. "Swallow every fucking drop he gives you."

That was all she needed. She redoubled her efforts, her head bobbing frantically now, a slave to his rhythm. Tim's body went rigid. A guttural shout tore from his throat, echoing off the concrete pillars.

He held her head still, buried to the hilt, as he emptied his load. Jean's throat worked, swallowing again and again, her eyes squeezed shut. When he finally pulled out, his cock was spent, glistening with her spit and his cum. A thick strand of it clung to her lower lip.

She stayed on her knees, panting, catching her breath. She wiped her mouth with the back of her hand, then looked at the mess on it. Slowly, deliberately, she licked her fingers clean, her eyes never leaving his.

Tim was slumped against the SUV, breathing hard. "Holy fuck."

I stepped forward, finally unzipping my own jeans, freeing my aching cock. "My turn," I said.

CHAPTER 5
Discovery in the Parking Ramp

The sound of my zipper was loud in the sudden quiet. Tim was still catching his breath, his softening cock glistening in the low light. Jean rose from her knees, a sly, filthy smile on her spit-slicked lips. She looked from my hard, waiting cock to Tim's slumped form.

"Don't get too comfortable," she purred, her voice hoarse. "We're just getting started."

She sauntered over to Tim's car, the black SUV, and leaned against the hood, her palms flat on the cool metal. The green dress was rumpled, her tits nearly free. She looked at Tim over her shoulder, the invitation clear.

Tim pushed off the SUV, a new hunger in his eyes. "You've got a hell of a woman, man," he said to me, but he was already moving toward her.

"I know," I said, my fist closing around my own aching cock. I gave it a slow, firm stroke. "And I love watching her."

Tim's hands landed on Jean's hips. He spun her around and pressed a rough, claiming kiss to her mouth. I saw her tongue dart out, tasting herself and him mixed together. Then he turned her back around, his movements deliberate and powerful.

"Bend over that hood, you filthy fucking tease," Tim growled, his voice raw.

Jean obeyed. She leaned forward, her palms squeaking on the metal. The position arched her back and made her ass a perfect, round offering. The hem of her dress was already high. Tim's hands gathered the fabric, yanking it up to her waist in one swift motion. She wasn't wearing panties. *Fuck. She'd planned this.*

Her pussy was exposed to the cool garage air, to Tim's gaze, and to mine. It was glistening, her lips puffy and wet, a darker pink against her skin. The scent of her arousal, musky and sweet, hit me even from a few feet away.

"Look at that," I breathed, stroking myself faster. "Look at her fucking cunt, Tim. It's dripping for you. It's been dripping the whole time she was sucking your cock."

Tim didn't waste time. He dropped to his knees behind her. His hands spread her cheeks apart, exposing everything—her swollen, needy pussy and the tight, pink furl of her asshole.

"You're fucking soaked," he muttered, his voice full of awe.

Then he leaned in and *licked*.

A long, flat, possessive stroke from her clit all the way back. Jean cried out, a sharp, beautiful sound that echoed. Her knuckles went white on the hood.

"Tell him what he's doing," I commanded, my own hand a blur on my cock.

"He's... he's licking my pussy," Jean moaned, her head dropping. "His tongue is so fucking *broad*. He's... oh, god... he's eating me out like he's fucking starving for it."

Tim was. He buried his face between her legs, his tongue spearing inside her, then circling her clit, then lapping at her like a man dying of thirst. The sounds were obscene—wet, sloppy, hungry. *Schlick. Slurp. Gulp.* He was devouring her.

Jean's moans became broken, pleas. "*Yes*... right there... suck on it... *suck on my fucking clit, you bastard!*"

Tim grunted, his hands gripping her ass hard enough to leave marks. He obeyed, sucking the little bud into his mouth, flicking it with the tip of his tongue. Jean's legs started to shake. I saw her hips trying to grind back against his face, fucking herself on his tongue.

"Is he good?" I asked, my own balls drawing up tight just from watching.

"He's… he's fucking *amazing*," she sobbed. "His tongue… it's so fucking *rough*… I can feel every ridge… he's gonna make me come… Aaron, he's going to make me come with his fucking mouth!"

"Do it," I snarled. "Come all over his face. Let him taste it."

Her orgasm hit her like a truck. Her back arched violently, a scream tearing from her throat that was half-pain, half-bliss. She shook, her entire body convulsing as Tim kept licking, drinking every drop she gave him. He didn't stop until her tremors subsided into weak shudders.

He stood up, wiping his mouth with the back of his hand. His cock was hard again, thick and angry-looking. He rubbed the head through Jean's wetness, coating himself in her juices.

"Are you ready for this?" He asked her, his voice thick.

Jean, still panting, pushed her ass back toward him. "Fuck me. Fuck me *hard*. I want to feel you in my guts."

He didn't need to be asked twice. He positioned himself, the broad head of his cock nudging against her entrance. He looked at me, a challenge in his eyes. I gave him a single, sharp nod.

Then he *shoved*.

He buried himself in one deep, brutal thrust.

Jean screamed again, a raw, ragged sound of absolute fullness. Her hands slipped on the hood.

"*Fuck!*" she cried. "Oh, fuck, it's so *deep*!"

He was. I could see how much of him was still outside, but what was inside her was stretching her impossibly wide. He began to move. No gentle rhythm. This was a fucking. Hard, driving, punishing strokes that slammed her body into the car with every thrust. The SUV rocked on its suspension. *Thump. Thump. Thump.*

The sound of skin slapping against skin filled the garage, mixing with their grunts and her screams.

"Do you feel that, you filthy slut?" Tim grunted, his hands like vices on her hips. "You feel my fat fucking cock splitting you open?"

"Yes!" Jean wailed, her face turned toward me, her expression a mask of ecstatic agony. "I feel it! I feel all of it! *Fuck me!*"

I matched my strokes to Tim's rhythm, my fist a tight tunnel around my own cock. Precum leaked over my fingers. I was so close, just from watching. Watching her take it. Watching her love it.

"Tell me what you want, Jean," I demanded, my voice guttural.

"I want… I want him to fuck my pussy raw!" she sobbed, her words breaking with each powerful thrust. "I want him to… to pound my fucking cunt until I can't walk! I want you to *watch* him ruin me!"

Tim was relentless. He was fucking her with a single-minded focus, his body a piston, his cock a battering ram. Sweat gleamed on his back. Jean's curls were stuck to her forehead. The hood of the car was warm from their heat.

"Are you going to come again?" Tim growled, his pace becoming frantic and erratic. "Are you going to come on this stranger's cock while your man jacks off?"

"Yes! *Yes!*" she screamed, her body tightening. "I'm coming! I'm fucking *coming!*"

Her second climax ripped through her. She clamped down on him, her inner muscles milking his cock. Tim saw it and felt it. He lost his rhythm. With a final, brutal slam, he buried himself to the hilt and held there. His body went rigid, a roar tearing from his lungs.

He was coming inside her. Pumping his load deep into her used, stretched, dripping cunt.

The sight of it, the *knowledge* of it, was my undoing. My own orgasm exploded up my spine. My cock pulsed in my hand, streaks of hot cum shooting onto the concrete floor between my feet. I groaned, my legs weak, my eyes locked on the place where Tim was still joined to Jean, where his seed was spilling out of her around the base of his cock.

Tim slumped over her, both of them breathing in ragged, shattered gasps. He slowly pulled out.

The aftermath was obscene. A thick, white trickle of his cum immediately began to seep out of her, sliding down her inner thigh. She was gaping, beautifully, ruinously open.

Jean slowly pushed herself up on trembling arms. She turned her head, her eyes finding mine, glazed and sated. A slow, wicked smile touched her bruised lips.

"Your turn, baby," she whispered.

CHAPTER 6

Discovery in the Hot Tub

The garage air, thick with the smell of sex and engine oil, seemed to cling to us as we walked. We sent Tim back to the bar with a slap on the back and a promise that his next bourbon was on my tab. He staggered off, a dazed, fucked-out grin on his face, a man who'd gotten far more than he'd bargained for at a hotel bar.

Jean leaned into me, her heat seeping through my clothes. She could feel the slickness between her thighs, a wet patch of Tim's spent cum coating her inner skin, a filthy secret she carried through the sterile lobby. The cool, conditioned air was a shock against their feverish skin.

"Let's go to the hot tub," Jean murmured, her voice still ragged from being throat-fucked. "I could use a good soak. I need to feel that hot water on my… well, on everything."

We didn't speak in the elevator up to our room. The silence was heavy with what we'd just done, what we'd shared. In our room, we peeled off our clothes. I watched her step out of that gorgeous green dress, now rumpled and stained. She stood naked before me, proud, her full tits jiggling slightly, her curly hair a wild mess, and that glorious, creamy mess of Tim's load glistening on her pussy and thighs. *Fuck, she was a vision.*

We pulled on our swimsuits, hers a flimsy pretense of modesty, and headed down to the pool deck. The air was humid and smelled of chlorine. The hot tub, a large, bubbling cauldron, was set in a dimly lit corner. And it was occupied.

A couple, maybe our age, was already submerged in the churning water. The man, Robert, had a head of silver hair and a confident, relaxed posture. The woman, Susan, was softer, with kind eyes and a smile that didn't quite hide a glint of mischief. We exchanged the obligatory polite nods as we slipped into the opposite side of the tub.

The water was blissfully, almost painfully hot after the garage's chill. It enveloped us, and I sighed, leaning my head back against the rim. Jean settled beside me, her leg brushing mine under the water. The bubbles roared, a constant, churning froth that hid everything below the surface.

We made small talk. The conference. The city. The hotel. Robert was in pharmaceuticals. Susan was a consultant. It was all mundane, a stark, surreal contrast to the raw filth they'd just been wallowing in. Jean played her part perfectly, the charming, slightly tipsy girlfriend, but I felt the energy shifting. Her foot found mine again, this time tracing a slow circle on my ankle.

Then I felt it.

A touch. Not Jean's.

A hand, soft and deliberate, landed on my thigh under the cover of the furious bubbles. My eyes snapped open. Susan was looking right at me, her expression unchanged as she continued her conversation with Jean about spa treatments. But her hand… her hand was moving. It slid slowly up my inner thigh, her fingers kneading the muscle there.

A jolt of pure electricity shot straight to my cock, which began to harden instantly against the fabric of my swim trunks. I didn't move. I didn't dare breathe. I just looked at her, and she gave me the faintest, most wicked smirk.

Her fingers crept higher, tracing the outline of my rapidly thickening shaft through the wet material. I bit down on my lip, my heart hammering against my ribs. Jean was watching me now, a slow, knowing smile spreading across her face. She'd seen the change in my posture, the dilation of my pupils. She knew.

"You okay, honey?" Jean asked, her voice dripping with fake innocence.

"Peachy," I managed to grunt, just as Susan's clever fingers found the waistband of my trunks. She didn't hesitate. She slipped her hand inside, her cool fingers a shocking contrast to the hot water as they wrapped around my bare, rock-hard cock.

Oh, fuck.

My head fell back against the rim with a soft thud. I closed my eyes, surrendering to the sensation. Robert was still talking, completely oblivious to the fact that his wife's hand was firmly wrapped around another man's straining erection just inches away.

Susan began to stroke. It wasn't tentative or shy. It was confident, expert. Her fist moved up and down my shaft with a slow, relentless rhythm, her thumb swirling over the slick head with every upstroke, smearing my own pre-cum. The water and the bubbles provided a perfect, slick lubricant, making every movement sinful and smooth.

"So, Aaron," Robert said, and I forced my eyes open. "Jean tells me you're in tech."

"Yeah," I breathed, my voice tight. "Data... uh... data security." Susan's grip tightened fractionally, and she gave me a slow, deliberate pull that made my toes curl.

"Fascinating," Robert said, and I had to stifle a groan.

Jean leaned closer, pretending to adjust her swimsuit top. "*Is she good?*" she whispered directly into my ear, her breath hot. "*Is her hand on your fucking cock right now?*"

"*Yes*," I hissed back, my hips giving a tiny, involuntary thrust into Susan's fist.

"*Tell me what she's doing*," Jean commanded, her own hand slipping under the water to find my leg, her nails digging in. "*Tell me exactly how her fucking hand feels on you.*"

I was caught between two women, my wife urging me on while a stranger jacked me off under the water. It was the most deliriously fucking erotic situation of my life.

"She's... fuck... she's got a firm grip," I whispered, my words barely audible over the bubbles. "Her fingers are wrapped around my shaft. She's pulling my skin back, her thumb is pressing right on the tip... right on the fucking slit... *god*damn it..."

Susan increased her pace, her wrist moving faster, her fingers working my cock with a knowing pressure that told him she'd done this before. Her other hand joined, cupping my balls under the water, rolling them gently in her palm. The dual sensation was unbelievable. I was a live wire, every nerve ending screaming.

"She's playing with my balls, Jean," I moaned, not caring who heard. "She's massaging them while she jerks my fucking cock. I can feel her wedding ring... It's cold against my skin."

Jean's eyes were dark with lust. "*You like that? You like another man's wife giving you a handjob in a public hot tub while he sits three feet away?*"

"I fucking love it," I gasped. My breathing was becoming ragged. I was hurtling toward the edge, my abs clenching, my thighs tensing. "I'm not gonna last… Susan… *fuck*…"

Susan's eyes met mine. She saw my impending climax. She smiled, a genuine, turned-on smile this time, and gave her husband's arm a casual squeeze with her free hand, all while the other one milked my cock with frantic, desperate strokes.

"I think we might head up soon, dear," she said to Robert, her voice perfectly even. "It's getting late."

"Sure thing," he replied.

And that was all it took. The sheer audacity, the filth of it, pushed me over. My orgasm ripped through me, violent and silent. My back arched, my mouth opened in a soundless scream as I came, jets of hot cum pulsing into the churning water, swallowed instantly by the sanitizing chemicals and the bubbles. Susan never stopped, working me through every last shuddering spasm, milking me completely dry until I was a trembling, spent heap against the tub wall.

She slowly, gently, withdrew her hand from my trunks. She brought it up above the water and pretended to adjust her hair, giving me one last, smoldering look.

Jean squeezed my thigh, her expression one of triumphant, shared deviance. "Feel better, baby?" she asked, loud enough for everyone to hear.

I could only nod, my breath still coming in short gasps.

Robert stood up, water sluicing off him. "Well, it was a pleasure meeting you both," he said, completely unaware of the torrent of orgasm his wife had just orchestrated just beside him.

Susan stood too, a serene smile on her face. "Yes, a real pleasure."

As they stepped out of the tub, she turned back, her eyes locking with mine.

"Maybe we'll see you around tomorrow."

CHAPTER 7
Discovery in the Garden

The garden was a world away from the garage's grit and the hot tub's chlorine steam. Twinkling fairy lights were strung through the trees, and the air was thick with the scent of night-blooming jasmine. Jean's hand was warm in mine, her body swaying close as we walked the manicured path. Her green dress was gone, replaced by a simple sundress, but the look in her eyes was the same: hungry, predatory, and utterly mine.

We found a secluded gazebo, shrouded in wisteria vines. It was private and romantic. The perfect place to decompress. I pulled Jean into my arms, my hands sliding down to cup the glorious curve of her ass. "Still sore?" I murmured into her hair.

She grinned against my chest. "In the best fucking way. I can still feel him. A deep, satisfying ache."

I was about to tell her how fucking hot that was when a young man, maybe twenty-five, approached. He was handsome in a clean-cut way, wearing the hotel's polo shirt. "Evening," he said, his smile easy. "Can I interest you in a cocktail? It will be on the house."

Jean's eyes lit up. "A house cocktail? Don't mind if we do."

"A mojito for Jean," I said, my voice steady, my eyes never leaving hers as she smirked, her lips curving into that mischievous smile he loved so much. "And I'd like a Weller Antique 107, neat."

Her grin widened, those familiar sparks of mischief dancing in her gaze. She leaned in slightly, her voice low and teasing. *"You know me so well."*

Jean turned to me, her smirk deepening, and I could feel the electricity between us crackling like a live wire. The air was thick with anticipation, and I knew she was already thinking ahead—her mind racing with possibilities. Her fingers traced a lazy pattern on my arm, her touch both teasing and grounding.

The young man nodded, his gaze lingering on Jean for a beat longer than necessary. There was *something* in his expression—a flicker of curiosity, maybe even intrigue—before he turned and disappeared back toward the main building. I caught it, and so did Jean. She leaned into me, her body warm against mine, her breath hot and teasing as it brushed my ear.

"You're quiet," she murmured, her voice low and sultry. "Thinking about what's next?"

I grinned, pulling her closer until her body pressed against mine. "Always." Her laugh was soft and knowing, and it sent a jolt of heat through me. We were alone in the garden, but the night was far from over.

"Weller 107? Feeling fancy tonight, are we?" She murmured, her voice low and dripping with playful seduction. But her eyes? They were fixed on the spot where the young man had been, a mischievous glint sparkling in them. She'd noticed it too—that little hint of something more behind his smile. And just like that, the air between us crackled with unspoken possibilities.

I chuckled, my hand slipping around her waist, pulling her closer. "Only the best for tonight," I murmured, my voice low. "Seems fitting, doesn't it?"

She laughed softly, her lips brushing my cheek before she pulled back, her eyes sparkling with anticipation. The night was far from over, and we both knew it.

We settled on the gazebo's built-in bench, my arm around her. The quiet was intimate, but the energy between us was still crackling from the night's exploits. I could smell a hint of Susan's chlorine and lust on my skin and Jean's mix of her own arousal and Tim's spent cum. We were a walking fucking crime scene of debauchery.

He returned quicker than we expected, carrying a tray with two glasses, Jean's garnished with mint. But he wasn't alone. A woman followed him. She was tall and statuesque, with skin the color of dark espresso and an aura of cool, collected authority. She wore a sleek black blazer and slacks, casual business attire that did nothing to hide the powerful, sensual curve of her hips and the impressive swell of her breasts beneath her silk shell.

The young man set the drinks down and melted away into the shadows. The woman stepped into the gazebo, her heels clicking softly on the wood. Her smile was not the polite smile of hotel staff. It was knowing. Penetrating.

"Good evening. I'm Ms. Adebayo," she said, her voice a low, melodic contralto that seemed to vibrate right into my bones. "I'm the property manager." She gestured to the drinks. "Please, enjoy."

Jean took a sip, her eyes never leaving the woman. I followed suit, raising the glass of Weller Antique to my lips. The bourbon was *strong*, with a bold, oaky tang that hit the back of my throat and lingered there, smoky and complex. It was rich, layered with hints of caramel and spice, just like the woman standing before us. Ms. Adebayo's presence was as intoxicating as the drink itself, her dark eyes watching us with a quiet, confident authority that demanded attention. Jean's lips curved into a sly smile as she leaned back, clearly enjoying more than just the cocktail.

The air in the gazebo felt charged, electric, as if the night still had more in store for them. Much more.

Ms. Adebayo folded her arms, and the movement pulled her blazer taut across her chest. "I hope you're enjoying your stay."

"Very much," Jean said, her voice a little breathy.

"I'm glad to hear it." She paused, her gaze drifting from Jean to me and back again. The air grew thick and charged. "Because I was reviewing some of our security footage earlier. Standard procedure. And I found something... fascinating."

My blood went cold for a second, then instantly hot. Jean's hand tightened on my thigh.

Ms. Adebayo's smile widened, a flash of perfect white teeth. "Oh, don't look so alarmed. Our cameras in the garage are primarily for liability. But their resolution is... exceptionally high." She let the words hang in the air, a blatant, delicious threat. "I was watching you two. With another guest. A Mr. Tim."

Fuck. She'd seen it all. Every slurp, every thrust, every scream.

Jean, my brave, filthy girl, recovered first. She leaned back, crossing her legs, letting her sundress ride up her thigh. "And?" she challenged, a defiant glint in her eye. "Did you enjoy the show?"

Ms. Adebayo's laugh was a rich, warm sound. "I found it utterly captivating. The trust. The raw... enthusiasm. The lack of inhibition." Her eyes roamed over Jean's body, then mine, with the appraisal of a connoisseur. "It's a rare thing to witness. It's an even rarer thing to possess."

She took a step closer. The jasmine scent was suddenly overpowered by her perfume, something dark and spicy, like old wood and desire. "I manage this property. I ensure discretion and satisfaction for all our guests. But my tastes... my personal interests... run toward the more *participatory*."

She was standing right in front of Jean now. She reached out, and with a single, elegantly manicured finger, she traced the line of Jean's jaw. Jean shivered, a full-body tremor, and her lips parted in a silent gasp.

"You have a mouth made for sin," Ms. Adebayo said, her voice dropping to an intimate murmur meant only for us. "I watched it stretch around that man's very average cock. I watched you swallow his pathetic, salty load." Her finger trailed down Jean's neck, over her collarbone, and came to rest just above the neckline of her dress, right between her tits. "I found myself thinking... what a waste of such a perfect canvas."

She turned her smoldering gaze to me, her dark eyes locking onto mine with an intensity that made my pulse quicken. "And you," she began, her voice a low, velvety purr that seemed to wrap itself around me. "The silent director. The voyeur who pulls the strings. I saw the look on your face when she swallowed. You weren't jealous. You weren't angry. No, you were *proud*." She paused, letting the weight of her words sink in, her lips curving into a knowing smile. "That's rare, you know. Most men would be seething, their egos bruised. But not you. You relished it. You were in complete control, and yet you let her take the lead, let her shine. It was... fascinating."

I felt a slow heat rise in my chest, a mixture of pride and arousal. She was right—every word of it. I had never felt jealousy watching Jean with Tim. Instead, I had felt a deep, visceral satisfaction, a thrill that came from seeing her so free, so unapologetically herself. Ms. Adebayo's gaze held mine, unflinching, as if she could see every thought, every fantasy that had played out in my mind as I watched Jean devour Tim in the garage. "You're a rare breed," she continued, her voice dropping to a whisper that felt like a secret shared between just the two of us. "A man who doesn't just tolerate his woman's desires but *celebrates* them. That's power. And it's intoxicating."

Her words hung in the air like a challenge, like an invitation. I could feel Jean's eyes on me too, her breath shallow, her body still trembling faintly from Ms. Adebayo's touch. The tension between the three of us was palpable, a thick, electric current that made the hairs on the back of my neck stand on end. Ms. Adebayo stepped closer, her perfume enveloping me, spicy and heady, and her voice dropped even lower, almost conspiratorial. "I can see it in you," she murmured. "The hunger. The need to watch, to control, to surrender all at once. You're not just a voyeur. You're a willing participant in her pleasure. And that... that makes you dangerous."

Her words sent a shiver down my spine, a rush of heat pooling low in my gut. I glanced at Jean, her eyes wide, her lips parted, and I knew she felt it too—the undeniable pull of this woman, the way she could unravel us both with just a few carefully chosen words. Ms. Adebayo smiled again, slow and predatory, and I wondered just how far she was willing to take this, how much more of ourselves we were about to give her. The night was no longer ours; it was hers. And we were nothing more than eager players in her game.

Ms. Adebayo reached out again, her fingers tracing Jean's collarbone. A slight, involuntary shudder from Jean told them both that more than just a moment was being shared.

CHAPTER 8
Discovery in the Gazebo

Ms. Adebayo's finger stayed pressed between Jean's tits, a silent claim. Jean's breathing was shallow, her eyes wide and dark with want. The manager's gaze flicked to me, a question in her dark eyes. I gave a single, slow nod. *Do it.*

That was all the permission she needed.

She cupped Jean's face with both hands, her touch surprisingly tender for a moment before it turned possessive. She leaned in, and their lips met.

It wasn't a tentative kiss. It was deep, *hungry*, and fucking loud. A moan tore from Jean's throat the second their mouths connected. Ms. Adebayo's tongue plunged inside, and Jean surrendered to it completely, her hands coming up to clutch at the woman's blazer. I watched, my cock hardening painfully against my zipper, as the two women devoured each other. The sounds were filthy—wet sucks, soft gasps, and the slick slide of tongue on tongue.

Ms. Adebayo broke the kiss, trailing her mouth down Jean's jaw to her neck. "You taste like sin and fresh mint," she murmured against Jean's skin, her voice a rasp. "I'm going to taste the rest of you."

Her hands went to the thin straps of Jean's sundress. With a sharp tug, they slid down Jean's shoulders. The dress pooled at her waist, exposing her full, beautiful tits to the warm night air. Ms. Adebayo's breath hitched. "Exquisite," she whispered, before taking one nipple into her mouth.

Jean cried out, her back arching, pushing her nipple deeper into that hot, sucking mouth. Ms. Adebayo's hand found Jean's other breast, kneading the soft flesh, pinching the nipple between her fingers. Jean's head fell back, her eyes finding mine. They were glazed, pleading, *owning* me with her pleasure.

"Aaron... *fuck*..."

"Watch her, baby," I said, my voice rough. "Watch her suck your tits."

Ms. Adebayo switched to the other nipple, lavishing it with the same brutal attention. Her free hand slid down Jean's stomach, over the curve of her belly, and under the bunched fabric of her dress. I saw her fingers disappear. Jean's eyes slammed shut, a choked gasp escaping her.

"She's so wet," Ms. Adebayo announced, her voice muffled against Jean's breast. "Her cunt is *dripping*. Is this for me? Or for him?"

"For... for both of you," Jean panted.

Ms. Adebayo straightened up, her lips glistening. She looked at me, her gaze burning. "Take your clothes off."

The command in her voice went straight to my dick. I didn't hesitate. I shoved my jeans and boxers down in one frantic motion, kicking them aside. My cock sprang free, thick and achingly hard. Ms. Adebayo's eyes dropped to it, and a slow, approving smile spread across her face.

"Good," she purred. She turned back to Jean, gripping the hem of her sundress. "Lift your hips."

Jean did, and Ms. Adebayo peeled the dress off her, tossing it onto the gazebo bench. Jean was naked now, bathed in the soft fairy light, her skin glowing. Ms. Adebayo guided her to turn around and bend over the wooden railing of the gazebo. Jean obeyed, presenting her ass to us—the same ass that had been fucked raw by a stranger just hours before.

Ms. Adebayo ran a hand over the lush curve of Jean's cheek, then gave it a sharp, stinging slap. Jean yelped, then moaned, pushing back for more.

"Such a greedy, used little thing," Ms. Adebayo said, her voice thick with lust. She looked at me over Jean's back. "You want to fuck her? Or do you want to watch me fuck her first?"

The choice was a devil's bargain. I stepped forward, my hand wrapping around the base of my cock. "I want to watch you make her scream."

Ms. Adebayo's smile was victorious. She quickly unbuttoned her slacks, pushing them and her underwear down just enough to free herself. I hadn't known what to expect, but the sight of the sleek, black strap-on harness and the realistic, thick silicone cock it held made my mouth go dry. It was *big*. Bigger than mine. Bigger than Tim's.

She took a small bottle from her blazer pocket—lube—and slicked the fake cock until it shone. She positioned herself behind Jean, the head nudging against Jean's soaked, puffy lips.

"You want this inside you, you filthy exhibitionist?" Ms. Adebayo growled.

"*Yes!*" Jean sobbed, pushing her hips back. "Please, fuck me with it!"

"Ask your man. He's the one who lets you be this way."

Jean turned her head, her cheek pressed against the wood. Her eyes, swimming with tears of need, locked on mine. "Aaron... please... let her fuck me. Let her stretch my cunt open with her big fucking cock. I need it. I *need* it so bad."

Her words were a fire in my blood. "Do it," I commanded, my hand stroking my own dick in time with my words. "Fuck her hard. Make her feel it tomorrow."

Ms. Adebayo pushed.

The head of the toy pressed inside, stretching Jean's entrance. Jean's mouth opened in a silent scream, her knuckles white on the railing. Ms. Adebayo leaned over her, one hand braced on Jean's back, the other guiding her fake cock. She pushed deeper, an inexorable, slow invasion.

"*Oh, god... oh, fuck...*" Jean chanted, her voice breaking.

I watched, mesmerized, as inch after thick, silicone inch disappeared into my wife's cunt. Ms. Adebayo didn't stop until her hips were flush against Jean's ass, the entire length buried to the hilt. Jean was *full*, stuffed to the brink.

"Look at her take it," Ms. Adebayo hissed, her own breath coming fast. "Look at her hungry little cunt swallowing every inch."

Then she pulled back and slammed home.

The impact was brutal. Jean's whole body jolted. A ragged cry tore from her throat. Ms. Adebayo set a punishing pace immediately, fucking Jean with long, powerful strokes that drove her into the railing with every thrust. The wet, slapping sounds of flesh on flesh, of silicone plunging into slick, tight heat, filled the quiet garden.

"You like that, you whore?" Ms. Adebayo grunted, her composure slipping into raw, dominant need. "You like getting your pussy fucked by another woman while your man watches?"

"Yes! "*Fuck, yes!*" Jean screamed. "It's so *deep*! It's hitting... it's hitting *everything*!"

I couldn't take it anymore. I moved behind Ms. Adebayo, my cock nudging against the cleft of her ass, still covered by her silky underwear. She glanced back, her eyes wild. "Do it," she snarled. "Fuck my ass while I fuck your woman's cunt."

I spit into my hand, slicked myself, and pushed her panties aside. Her asshole was tight, a small, puckered rosebud. I pressed the head of my cock against it, applying steady pressure. She was tight, *so* fucking tight, but with a groan she pushed back, taking me inside.

The sensation was insane. I was buried in the hot, clenching tightness of her ass, my body pressed against her back, and in front of me, she was fucking Jean senseless with a rubber cock. We were a chain of lust, a filthy, connected circuit.

I started to move, my hips pistoning against her ass. At first, the rhythm was awkward, then we found it—a syncopated, brutal rhythm. I'd thrust into Ms. Adebayo's ass, and the force would drive her forward, plunging the toy even deeper into Jean.

Jean was unraveling. Her pleas became wordless screams. Her cunt was gushing, her juices coating the toy and dripping down her thighs. Ms. Adebayo reached around, her fingers finding Jean's clit, rubbing furious, tight circles.

"I'm gonna come!" Jean shrieked. "I'm gonna come on her fucking cock!"

"Come, dear, do it," I grunted, slamming into Ms. Adebayo's ass, feeling my own orgasm coiling at the base of my spine. "Scream for us."

Jean's body locked up. A soundless scream contorted her face as her orgasm detonated. Her cunt clamped down on the toy in violent, rhythmic pulses. The force of it made Ms. Adebayo cry out, her own body shuddering. Feeling her convulse around my cock was my undoing. I buried myself to the hilt in her ass and let go, my cum erupting in hot, pumping waves deep inside her.

We collapsed forward in a heap, a sweaty, panting, cum-slicked tangle of limbs on the gazebo floor. The toy slid out of Jean with a wet, obscene sound. I pulled out of Ms. Adebayo, both of us groaning at the separation.

For a long moment, there was only the sound of our ragged breathing and the distant hum of the city. Ms. Adebayo was the first to move. She disentangled herself, pulling up her slacks with surprisingly steady hands. She looked down at us, Jean sprawled bonelessly, me propped on an elbow, both of us covered in the evidence of what we'd just done.

Her expression was one of supreme, satisfied calm. She smoothed her blazer.

"That was... an adequate appetizer," she said, her voice back to its cool, managerial melody. She reached into her inner blazer pocket and produced two small, black cards, handing one to Jean and one to me.

"We have a special event tomorrow evening," she said, her eyes glinting in the low light. "There will be a few couples and many single men. I would love to have Jean as the center of attention." She looked directly at me. "Aaron, you will have plenty to do as well, of course. It is a masked affair. Completely anonymous."

She let that hang in the air, a promise and a threat.

"If you are willing to come," she finished, a slow smile spreading on her lips, "I will comp your stay with us."

CHAPTER 9
Discovery Masked

The deep red robe felt lush against my fingers, the white fur trim soft as a cloud. It hung loose on Jean's curvy frame, tied with a simple silk sash. My own costume—a dark Victorian tailcoat, crisp white shirt, and fitted trousers—felt stiff and formal. A barrier. Jean's costume was an invitation.

Ms. Adebayo herself fastened the final touch: a hood of the same red velvet, drawn over Jean's curly hair. It fastened under her chin, completely covering her eyes. "So she can be truly present in her body," Ms. Adebayo murmured, her voice a velvet promise. She handed me a simple black half-mask. "And so you can watch without inhibition."

Jean's hand found mine, her grip tight. I could feel the fine tremble in her fingers. "It will be okay, my dear," I whispered, lifting her knuckles to my lips. "I'm right here with you."

Ms. Adebayo led us through a service corridor we hadn't known existed, then through a heavy, unmarked door. The air changed instantly. Cool, dry, and smelling of beeswax, perfume, and a faint, musky anticipation. We entered a vast, private ballroom.

It was dim, lit only by hundreds of flickering candles in sconces and on low tables. Shadows danced on dark wood-paneled walls. Soft, baroque chamber music floated from hidden speakers. And there were people. Dozens of them, standing in quiet groups or lounging on divans. All wore masks—intricate lace, sleek leather, glittering metallic. Men in fine suits, women in elegant, revealing gowns. A low murmur of conversation hummed in the space, stopping briefly as we entered.

All those masked faces turned toward Jean.

She squeezed my hand harder, her breath catching. I put my arm around her shoulders, pulling her close. "Just breathe," I whispered into her hood. "You're the most beautiful thing in this room."

Ms. Adebayo glided ahead, turning to address the assembled guests. Her voice, clear and commanding, cut through the music. "My friends. Our canvas has arrived."

She gestured to a raised, circular platform in the very center of the room, lit by a soft, downward spotlight. It was covered in what looked like dark velvet. A dais. A stage.

My heart hammered against my ribs. This was it. I led Jean forward, her steps hesitant but trusting. We ascended two shallow steps to the platform. The room was utterly silent now. I turned Jean to face me, my hands on her shoulders. I could see nothing of her expression, just the soft curve of her lips below the hood's edge. I leaned in, kissing her deeply, pouring every ounce of my pride and filthy excitement into it. She moaned into my mouth, her tongue tangling with mine.

Then, my fingers went to the silk sash at her waist. I untied it. The robe fell open. I pushed it back from her shoulders, letting the heavy fabric slide down her arms, over the full swell of her breasts, and down the curve of her belly to puddle at her feet on the velvet.

She stood naked in the spotlight. Her skin glowed. Her nipples were already hard, pebbled tight. A soft, awed sigh seemed to ripple through the watching crowd.

I stepped back, down to the floor, leaving her alone on the dais. I raised my voice, letting it ring out clear and strong. "She is yours, ladies and gentlemen! Do as you please!"

For a heartbeat, nothing happened. Then, movement.

A woman emerged first. She wore a silver mask and a sheer black gown. She climbed the steps and walked a slow circle around Jean, her eyes devouring her. Then she stopped behind her, her hands sliding around Jean's waist, cupping her heavy breasts. Jean gasped, her head tipping back. The woman pinched her nipples hard, rolling them between her fingers. Jean cried out, a sharp, needy sound.

A man followed. He was broad-shouldered, masked like a fox. He knelt in front of Jean, his hands spreading her thighs apart. He didn't hesitate. He buried his face between her legs, his tongue licking a long, firm stripe up her slit.

"Oh, *fuck*!" Jean screamed, her knees buckling. The woman behind her held her up, still pinching and pulling at her tits.

I watched, my cock throbbing painfully against the fine wool of my trousers. I was so hard my cock felt like a separate entity, demanding release. Then, soft hands were on me. A woman with a feathered mask appeared at my side, her fingers deftly unbuttoning my fly. Another woman, her red hair spilling over a jeweled mask, knelt before me. They worked in tandem. One pulled my cock free; the other took it into her hot, wet mouth without a word.

Holy shit. I groaned, my head falling back. Her mouth was incredible, her tongue swirling around the head before she swallowed me deep, taking my entire length down her throat. The other woman kissed my neck, her hands sliding inside my shirt, teasing my nipples. I was being consumed, just as Jean was.

On the dais, the fox-masked man was eating at Jean's cunt like a starving man. I could hear the wet, sloppy sounds of his mouth on her pussy. Her legs were shaking. The silver-masked woman turned Jean's head and kissed her, swallowing her moans.

Then a third figure, a man in a simple black mask, approached. He unbuckled his pants, freeing a thick, rigid cock. He stepped up behind the kneeling man and simply pushed the fox-masked man aside. He positioned himself at Jean's dripping entrance and pushed inside in one smooth, powerful thrust.

Jean's scream was muffled by the woman's kiss. Her body bowed, taking the invasion. He started to fuck her, deep, rhythmic strokes that made her tits jounce wildly in the other woman's hands. The man on his knees didn't leave; he just moved lower, his tongue now lapping at her anus as the other man pounded into her soaking wet cunt.

The woman sucking me redoubled her efforts, her hand cupping my balls, squeezing in time with her sucks. The other woman had my shirt open now, her mouth on my chest, her teeth grazing my skin. Pleasure coiled, tight and hot, at the base of my spine. I couldn't look away from Jean.

Another man, this one with the lean build of a dancer, took the silver-masked woman's place. He pinched Jean's nipples brutally, twisting them. "You like being our little fuck-doll, don't you?" he growled.

"Yes! *God, yes!*" Jean sobbed, her voice raw.

The man fucking her pulled out, his cock glistening with her juices. The dancer rolled her onto her hands and knees on the velvet. He mounted her from behind immediately, slamming his own cock into her well-stretched cunt. The rhythm was brutal and frantic. The first man now stood before her face, feeding his cock between her lips. Jean took him eagerly, her mouth stretching wide, sucking him deep with hungry, noisy gulps.

She was being used from both ends, a beautiful, willing vessel. Her back was arched, her ass in the air, and her cunt was taking a pounding while her throat was fucked. A second woman climbed onto the dais, kneeling beside Jean's head. She gathered Jean's curly hair, holding it back, whispering encouragement as Jean choked and gagged on the cock in her mouth.

The sensation of the mouth on my cock, the hands on my body, the overwhelming sight before me—it was too much. "I'm going to come," I grunted.

The woman on her knees pulled off my cock with a wet pop and stroked me furiously with her hand. The other woman kissed me, her tongue fucking my mouth. "Come for her," she whispered against my lips. "Come watching your slut."

My orgasm ripped through me. I shouted, my hips bucking as I painted the kneeling woman's hand and chest with hot, pulsing streaks of cum. I shook with the force of it, my eyes glued to Jean.

Just as my climax subsided, Jean's body went rigid. A guttural, choked scream erupted from around the cock in her mouth as her own orgasm shattered her. Her cunt clenched visibly around the cock pistoning into her, her juices soaking the man's thighs. He roared, pounding into her through her convulsions, before pulling out and spraying his cum across the small of her back.

The man at her mouth followed suit, grunting as he emptied himself down her throat. Jean swallowed desperately, her throat working, before collapsing forward onto the velvet, panting and covered in sweat and sperm. The woman who'd kissed me wiped her hands on a small towel and gently tucked my softening cock back into my trousers, buttoning me up with a smile. "Your turn is next, you know," she said, her eyes sparkling behind her mask.

Before I could respond, the room seemed to stir again. More men stepped forward, their masked faces gleaming in the candlelight. One wore a crown-like mask adorned with antlers; another had a sleek, featureless black mask that caught the light like polished obsidian. They moved with purpose, circling Jean like predators closing in on their prey.

Jean, still sprawled on the velvet dais, lifted her head weakly. She was breathing hard, her body glistening with sweat and the remnants of her previous use. The antlered man knelt beside her first, his calloused hand brushing over her trembling thigh. "Such a good girl," he murmured, his voice rough and low. He positioned himself above her, his thick cock already hard as he guided it to her lips. Jean opened her mouth obediently, taking him in with a muffled moan.

The second man, the one with the black mask, moved behind her, spreading her thighs apart. He pressed the tip of his cock against the slick entrance to her anus and thrust deep in one fluid motion. Jean gasped around the cock in her mouth, her body arching as she was filled again.

A third man joined, his mask resembling a raven's beak. He crouched between her legs, his tongue lashing at her clit while the other two men fucked her relentlessly. Jean's cries were muffled but desperate, her hips writhing as she tried to meet every thrust, every lick.

Then, more men appeared, their cocks hard and ready. They circled the dais, their hands stroking themselves as they watched Jean being used. One by one, they stepped forward, their releases painting her skin in thick streaks—her face, her breasts, and her belly. Jean's hooded head turned this way and that, her mouth open to catch as much as she could, her tongue darting out to lick at the streams of cum dripping down her chin.

By the time the last man finished, Jean was a masterpiece of debauchery, glistening under the spotlight like a canvas splattered with white paint. Her body heaved with each breath, chest rising and falling as she lay there, utterly spent.

The room fell into a hushed silence, broken only by the sound of her soft whimpers and the ticking of a distant clock.

The music swelled. The participants stepped back, melting into the shadows, adjusting their clothes. Jean lay spent and trembling on the dais.

Jean was a trembling, quivering mess. A beautifully painted canvas of lust. I went to her, took her in my arms, and said, "My dear, you were marvelous!" "No," Jean said. "The event was marvelous. It was everything I have dreamed it would be."

CHAPTER 10
Discovery with New Friends

Ms. Adebayo's voice cut through the hazy, satisfied silence that had settled over the ballroom. "For those who wish to continue the evening in a more... *intimate* setting, please follow me."

A low murmur of approval rippled through the remaining masked guests. Jean, still naked and gleaming under the spotlight, turned her hooded face toward the sound of her husband's voice. "Aaron?"

I was at her side in an instant, helping her to her feet. Her skin was hot to the touch, sticky in some places, slick in others. I found her robe and draped it over her shoulders, leaving it open. "We're going, my dear," I whispered, my own blood heating again just feeling the tremble in her limbs.

We followed a smaller group, maybe ten people, through another discreet door behind the dais. This led to a sumptuous, dimly lit lounge. Plush couches formed a loose circle around a huge, low ottoman covered in soft leather. A bar stocked with crystal decanters stood against one wall. The air was thick with the smell of sex, expensive whiskey, and perfume.

The masks were coming off now, discarded on side tables with soft clicks. Faces were revealed, flushed and smiling. I recognized none of them. Not until a man with silver hair, his arm around a soft-curved woman with a mischievous glint in her eye, turned from the bar with two drinks in hand.

My breath caught.

Robert. And Susan.

From the hot tub.

Susan's eyes met mine first. A slow, knowing smile spread across her lips. She leaned over and whispered something to Robert. He looked over, his expression shifting from relaxed conversation to sharp, predatory interest. He raised his glass in a silent toast.

Well, fuck me.

Jean, sensing my stillness, clutched my arm. "What is it?"

"Remember the couple from the hot tub?" I murmured, my cock already stirring against my trousers.

Before she could answer, Ms. Adebayo glided into the center of the room. "The rules are simple here. There are no rules. Enjoy each other."

It was like a starter's pistol. The pretense of anonymous formality dissolved. A woman with short-cropped black hair immediately pulled a man onto one of the couches, her hand diving into his pants. Another couple, both men, began kissing passionately by the bar. Jean and I reclined on a comfy sofa and took in the scene around us.

Robert and Susan moved toward us with purpose. Robert's gaze was locked on Jean, drinking in the sight of her disheveled, cum-streaked glory. Susan came straight to me, her hand landing flat on my chest.

"We never got a proper introduction last time," she purred, her fingers toying with the buttons of my shirt. "I'm Susan. And I've been thinking about that big cock of yours for days."

Her boldness was a fucking spark to tinder. I grabbed the back of her neck and pulled her into a kiss. It was hard and messy, all tongue and teeth. She moaned into my mouth, her body melting against mine.

I broke the kiss, breathing hard. "And your husband?"

She nodded toward Jean. Robert was standing before her, his hands gently pushing the robe completely off her shoulders. It fell to the floor. Jean stood naked before him, her head still hooded.

"You are a vision," Robert said, his voice reverent. He didn't touch her yet. He just looked, his eyes roaming over every curve, every mark. He turned to me. "May I?"

Jean, her voice hoarse from screaming, whispered, "Yes." I simply nodded affirmation.

Robert's hands came up to cup her full, heavy breasts. He weighed them in his palms, his thumbs brushing over her hard, abused nipples. Jean gasped. "They're perfect," he groaned. He bent his head and took one nipple deep into his mouth, sucking hard.

Jean cried out, her hands flying to his silver hair.

Susan's hands were on my belt, then my zipper. She freed my cock, her fingers wrapping around the shaft. "*Mmm*, just as thick as I remember," she sighed, stroking me slowly. "I want to taste you properly this time. No water. Just my mouth on your fucking cock."

She pushed me back into the deep cushions of the sofa. I fell back into it, and she dropped to her knees between my legs without another word. She licked a long, slow stripe from my balls all the way up to the tip, her eyes locked on mine. Then she took me into the wet, incredible heat of her mouth.

"*Fuck*, Susan," I grunted, my head falling back.

On the ottoman, Robert had laid Jean down on her back. He was kneeling between her spread thighs, his mouth working lower. He kissed her stomach, her hips, then buried his face in her cunt. Jean arched off the leather with a sharp cry, her hands scrambling for purchase.

Robert ate her pussy like a man possessed. I could hear the wet, sloppy sounds from across the room. His tongue was driving deep, then fluttering over her clit. Jean's legs shook, her heels digging into the ottoman.

"She's close already," Robert growled, coming up for air, his chin glistening. "She's so fucking sensitive. Who's going to make her come?"

Susan pulled off my cock with a pop. "I will." She stood up, leaving me throbbing and desperate. She walked to the ottoman, shed her dress in one smooth motion, and climbed over Jean's face. She lowered her dripping cunt onto Jean's mouth. "Make me come first, sweetheart. Lick my pussy."

Jean's hooded head lifted, her tongue finding Susan's folds eagerly. At the same time, Robert drove two fingers deep into Jean's cunt, curling them, fucking her with his hand while he went back to sucking her clit.

The sight was unreal. My partner being eaten out while she pleasured another woman, all in the middle of a debauched orgy. I stood up, my cock aching, and went to them.

Robert saw me coming. He pulled his fingers from Jean's sopping cunt and offered them to me. I sucked them clean, tasting Jean's musky, sweet tang mixed with the salt of other men. It was the filthiest thing I'd ever done.

"Fuck her," Robert commanded, moving aside. "She's begging for it. I can feel her cunt pulsing."

I didn't need to be told twice. I mounted the ottoman, gripping Jean's hips, and slammed my cock into her in one brutal thrust.

Jean screamed around Susan's pussy, the vibration making Susan moan loudly. Jean's cunt was a furnace, impossibly tight and wet, clenching around me in frantic waves. She was completely overwhelmed, being fucked in her mouth and her pussy at the same time.

I set a punishing rhythm, pounding into her, my balls slapping against her ass. "You like that, you filthy girl?" I grunted. "You like having your cunt stuffed while you lick another woman's pussy?"

Her answer was a guttural, choking moan of absolute bliss. Her hips bucked, trying to take me deeper. Susan was rocking against Jean's face, her hands braced on the ottoman, her head thrown back in ecstasy.

"I'm gonna come!" Susan shrieked. "Oh god, right there, *don't stop*!"

Robert, now naked, his own cock thick and hard, moved behind Susan. He spat into his hand, slicked himself, and pressed his cockhead against her asshole. "Take this too, you greedy slut," he growled, and pushed inside her.

Susan's eyes flew open, a strangled cry ripped from her throat as she was filled from behind. The chain was complete now. Robert was fucking Susan's ass, Susan was grinding on Jean's mouth, and I was fucking Jean's cunt raw.

The sounds were animalistic. Grunts, slaps, wet squelches, and high, keening cries. The other couples in the room had stopped to watch, some stroking themselves, others just staring in rapt voyeuristic hunger.

I could feel my orgasm building, a tsunami at the base of my spine. Jean's cunt was milking me, her inner muscles fluttering wildly. "I'm gonna fill you up, Jean," I snarled, my thrusts becoming ragged and uncontrolled. "I'm gonna pump my cum so deep into your used little pussy."

That sent her over the edge. Her body locked in a rigid arch, a silent, shuddering scream tearing through her as her orgasm exploded. Her cunt clamped down on my cock like a vise, squeezing the cum right out of me. With a roar, I buried myself to the hilt and erupted, jet after hot jet of my release flooding her depths.

My climax triggered Susan's. She convulsed above Jean, her cunt gushing as she cried out Robert's name. Robert, feeling her ass clench around him, roared his own release, pumping his cum into her ass.

We collapsed into a sweaty, panting heap on the ottoman, a tangled knot of limbs and spent desire. Robert pulled out of Susan with a soft groan. I slid from Jean's well-fucked cunt, my cum immediately leaking out of her onto the leather.

Susan rolled off Jean, who lay boneless, her hood askew, her lips swollen and glistening. Susan kissed me, deep and languid, sharing the taste of Jean and sex. "We should have done this sooner," she whispered.

Robert was stroking Jean's hair, his expression one of awed satisfaction. He looked at me, then at the other watching guests, his eyes gleaming with a new idea.

CHAPTER 11

Discovery Shared

The morning sun cut through a gap in the blackout curtains, painting a sharp stripe across the rumpled hotel sheets. My body ached in the most exquisite way, a symphony of deep, used muscles and lingering, ghostly touches. Jean was curled into my side, her head on my chest, her warm breath teasing across my skin. I was already half-hard, morning wood mingling with the vivid, filthy memories of the night. But then she stirred, her fingers tracing lazy patterns on my stomach.

"You're awake," she murmured, her voice a sleepy, sexy rasp.

"Mmhmm. Thinking about last night."

She tilted her head up, her eyes still heavy-lidded but sparkling with a wicked light. "Which part?"

I chuckled, my hand finding the lush curve of her hip. "All of it. But especially the end. With Robert and Susan."

Jean shifted, rolling onto her back beside me, staring up at the ceiling. A slow, dirty smile spread across her lips. "Oh, god, Aaron. That was... fucking *unreal*."

She turned her head to look at me, her expression turning serious, intensely focused. "Do you want me to tell you? Every single feeling?"

My cock, which had been merely interested, gave a painful, insistent throb against my thigh. It was like a steel rod trapped in the sheets. "Yes," I breathed. "Tell me everything."

She took a deep breath, her eyes drifting closed as if to better access the memory. "When Robert first put his mouth on my cunt... after everything that had already happened... I thought I'd be numb. But I wasn't. His tongue felt like *lightning*. It was so focused, so *mean*. Not like a lover trying to please me, but like a man trying to *consume* me. He was sucking my clit like he wanted to pull my soul out through it."

I groaned, my hand drifting down to wrap around my own cock, giving it a slow stroke. The pre-cum was already beading at the tip.

"And his fingers..." she continued, her voice dropping to a husky whisper. "When he pushed them inside me, I could feel how swollen and open my pussy was from all the other cocks. It felt huge and empty and aching. And then he filled it, curling his fingers right up against that spot deep inside me, and I just… I started to unravel right there. I was shaking; my legs were just trembling fucking meat."

She opened her eyes, looking at me, watching my hand work my cock. It spurred her on. "Then Susan sat on my face. Her pussy… god, it was so wet and hot, and she tasted so fucking *sweet* and musky. I could feel her folds against my lips, her clit right there for my tongue. And I could hear Robert, his voice all rough, telling me what a good slut I was for eating his wife's cunt while he fucked mine with his mouth."

"Fuck, Jean," I grunted, my strokes speeding up.

"But then you came over," she said, her eyes blazing. "And you sucked his fingers. You sucked *my* taste off his fingers. I heard you. That was the nastiest, most possessive thing I've ever heard. And I felt my cunt just *gush*. I was so wet for you right then. I needed your cock more than I've ever needed anything."

She rolled onto her side, facing me, her hand coming to rest on my chest. "And then you fucked me. Oh, god, Aaron. You filled me up so completely. After all those other men, your cock… it felt like *home*. But a dirty, clamoring, violent home. You pounded into me, and I could feel every ridge, every vein. I could feel my own slick juices and… and other men's cum making it a fucking slip 'n slide for you."

Her fingers trailed down my stomach, through my coarse hair, and her hand wrapped around mine on my cock. She took over, her grip firm and knowing. "And when Susan came on my face, I felt her whole body shudder. Her juices flooded my mouth. I swallowed it all. And Robert was fucking her tight little asshole right above me, and I could feel the vibrations through her body into mine."

She began to stroke me, a slow, sensual up-and-down that had my toes curling. "And then you... you told me you were going to fill up my used little pussy. And I lost it. My orgasm wasn't a wave, Aaron. It was a *quake*. It started in my cunt, this clenching, pulsing riot, and it shot out to my fingers and my toes and my scalp. I was screaming into Susan's pussy, my body just seizing up around your cock. I felt you get even harder, then I felt the hot pulse of your cum filling me, jet after fucking jet, so deep inside me I thought it would come out my throat."

Her hand tightened, her thumb swirling over the sensitive head of my cock, spreading the pre-cum. "And when you pulled out... I felt it. I felt your cum start to leak out of me, right there onto the leather. It was hot and thick, and it was *yours*. Marking me. Claiming me back after I'd been everyone's whore."

I was panting, my hips lifting off the mattress, fucking up into her tight fist. "Jesus, Jean."

"I loved it," she whispered fiercely, leaning in to nip at my earlobe. "I loved being their canvas. I loved being their fuck-doll. But I *loved* being your wife again at the end. I loved you flooding my filthy, well-fucked cunt with your seed."

Her other hand cupped my balls, rolling them gently, then tracing a finger back to the sensitive skin behind them. "Are you close, baby?"

"Yes," I gasped. "God, yes. Your hand... the things you're saying..."

"Tell me what you want me to do," she commanded, her voice pure sex. "Do you want me to jack your big, hard cock off all over my tits? Do you want me to make you come on my face, like all those men did? Or do you want to save it and fuck this sore, stretched-out pussy of mine one more time?"

The choice was torture. The visual of her covered, the feel of her still-swollen flesh... "Your hand," I grunted. "Just your hand. Make me come with your fucking hand while you talk to me."

"Mmm, I can do that," she purred. Her strokes became faster and more purposeful. Her other hand tweaked my nipple, hard. "You liked watching, didn't you? You liked seeing my mouth stretched wide around a stranger's cock. You liked seeing my asshole getting licked while I got fucked."

"Yes! *Fuck*, yes!"

"You liked seeing Robert's silver hair between my legs, his tongue in my cunt. You liked seeing Susan ride my face." Her voice was a relentless, nasty chant. "And it made your cock so hard. It's making you come right now, isn't it? You're going to spray your hot cum all over your stomach because your wife is a beautiful, filthy exhibitionist slut."

That was it. The coil snapped. With a ragged shout, my back arched off the bed. My cock erupted in her fist, thick ropes of pearly white cum shooting up to my chest, spattering across my skin in hot, wet stripes. She milked me through it, her hand not stopping until the last shuddering pulse was wrung from me.

I collapsed, breathless, spent. Jean brought her cum-slicked fingers to her lips and sucked them clean, her eyes locked on mine. "Mmm. Tastes like victory."

She leaned down and kissed me, deep and slow, letting me taste myself on her tongue. Then she nestled back into my side, her hand resting on my damp chest. "So," she said, her tone shifting to something lighter, but no less charged. "What's on the agenda for today?"

CHAPTER 12
Discovery Challenged

We were halfway through room service coffee when a thick, cream-colored envelope slid under our hotel room door.

Jean padded over, naked and unselfconscious, and picked it up. She turned it over, her brow furrowed. There was no stamp, no address. Just her name, *Jean*, written in a flowing, elegant script. She broke the simple wax seal—an imprint of a stag's head.

Inside was a single card of heavy stock.

You have been observed. You have been enjoyed. Your appetites are known. If you seek to explore further, to navigate the labyrinth of your own deepest desires, present this card at the concierge desk at midnight. Come alone. Or come together. The choice, and the challenges, will be yours.

—The Stag & Vixen Society

My heart hammered against my ribs. I looked at Jean. Her eyes were wide, her pupils blown with a dark, eager hunger. The coffee was forgotten.

"A labyrinth?" I said, my voice rough.

"Sexual challenges," she breathed, the card trembling slightly in her hand. She looked at me. "What do you think it means?"

"I think it means we're not done." I stood up, crossing the room to her. I took the card from her fingers, then cupped her cheek. "I think it means they saw everything last night, and they want to see what we'll do when we're really tested."

She leaned into my touch, her lips parting. "Do you want to go?"

"Do you?"

Her answer was to kiss me, hard and desperate. It was all the consent I needed.

The hotel lobby was deserted at five minutes to midnight, the usual bustle replaced by a silent, expectant hum. Jean wore a simple black slip dress that hugged every curve. I was in dark trousers and a shirt, feeling like we were headed to a very different kind of job interview.

The concierge, a young man with an impassive face, took the card without a word. His eyes flicked over it, then up to us. "Follow the red light," he said softly, nodding toward a discreet, arched hallway off the main lobby we'd never noticed before. A single, tiny crimson bulb glowed above the entrance.

The hallway led to a plain, industrial elevator. The doors sighed open at our approach. We stepped inside. There were no buttons. The doors closed, and we descended for what felt like a full minute.

When they opened, sound washed over us first. A low, throbbing bassline. The murmur of voices. The scent of expensive perfume, sweat, and something sharper—anticipation.

We were in an antechamber, all dark stone and velvet drapes. A woman in a sleek black bodysuit and a delicate stag mask stood before a heavy curtain. "Welcome," she said, her voice melodic. "The labyrinth is a journey of choice. Each corridor presents a door. Each door, a challenge. You may accept or decline. There is no penalty for declining, only the path not taken. Proceed only if you are in absolute agreement." Her eyes, dark behind the mask, held mine, then Jean's. "Do you understand?"

We nodded, wordless.

She pulled the curtain aside.

The space beyond was vast, a multi-level honeycomb of balconies and partitioned spaces overlooking a central sunken floor. It was dimly lit, bathed in shifting hues of crimson and indigo. People moved in the shadows, some masked, some not. And everywhere, there were doors. Simple, unmarked doors along winding corridors that branched off from the main space.

A man in a tailored suit, his face obscured by a simple black domino mask, approached us with two glasses of champagne. "An offering to start your journey," he said, handing them over. "The first corridor is straight ahead. Choose wisely."

Jean took a nervous sip. I drained mine, the bubbles sharp on my tongue. We moved forward, into the first dim corridor. Three identical doors stood on the left wall.

"Which one?" Jean whispered.

"The middle," I said, no logic behind it.

I turned the handle. The room inside was small, circular, and lit by a single spotlight. In the center was a kneeling bench, like a church pew. A note was pinned to it.

Kneel. Serve. The one who kneels may not speak. The one who watches may only command. Pleasure the first stranger who enters until they release.

My blood went hot. Jean read it, her breath catching. She looked at me, a question in her eyes. This was a direct order, a defined role. Before I could even answer, the door behind us opened.

A woman walked in. She was tall and willowy, with long auburn hair cascading over bare shoulders. She wore only a pair of high-waisted silk shorts. Her small, pert tits were bare, her nipples tight peaks. She closed the door and leaned against it, looking at Jean with a cool, appraising gaze.

"I'm the stranger," she said, her voice a smoky alto.

The challenge was clear. I looked at Jean. "Kneel," I said, my voice firm.

A shudder of pure excitement went through her. She moved to the bench, arranging her dress as she knelt on the padded leather. The woman sauntered forward, stopping just before Jean. She hooked her thumbs in the waistband of her shorts and pushed them down her hips, letting them fall to the floor. She was completely shaved, her cunt lips already glistening under the spotlight.

"You know what to do," I commanded Jean. "Serve her."

Jean didn't hesitate. She leaned forward, her hands coming up to hold the woman's hips steady. She pressed her face into the junction of her thighs, inhaling deeply. Then her tongue emerged, a pink stripe in the dim light, and she licked a long, slow path from the woman's tight asshole all the way up to her clit.

The woman gasped, her head falling back. "*Oh*... yes. Just like that."

Jean dove in. This wasn't the hungry, desperate cunt-eating of the night before. This was *service*. Precise, attentive, worshipful. She used the flat of her tongue to spread the woman's slickness, then focused the tip on her swollen clit, flicking it in tiny, rapid circles. Her nose was buried in the woman's pussy, breathing her in. One of Jean's hands slid around to cup the woman's ass, fingers digging into the soft flesh.

I stood against the wall, my cock rigid in my trousers, my role to observe and command. "Suck her lips into your mouth," I growled. "Taste her properly."

Jean obeyed, pulling the woman's outer lips into her mouth, sucking on them, letting her teeth graze the sensitive skin. The woman moaned, her hands tangling in Jean's curly hair, not forcing, just holding on.

"Fuck her with your tongue," I said. "Deep."

Jean's tongue stabbed forward, plunging into the woman's tight, wet hole. She fucked her with it, in and out, the wet, sloppy sounds filling the small room. The woman's thighs began to tremble. "I'm... I'm so close," she panted. "Right there, don't stop, please don't fucking stop..."

"Make her come, Jean," I said, my own voice tight with arousal. "Drink her fucking cum."

Jean doubled her efforts, her mouth a blur of motion, sucking the clit, fucking the hole, devouring every inch of the woman's pussy. The woman's back arched, a strangled, beautiful cry ripped from her throat. Her hips jerked forward, grinding against Jean's face as her orgasm hit. I saw the muscles in her stomach clench and saw Jean's throat work as she swallowed.

The woman sagged, breathless, her body glistening with sweat. She gently pushed Jean's head back. Jean's face was a glistening, wet mess, her lips swollen, her eyes glazed with submission and pride. The woman reached down and stroked Jean's cheek with a trembling hand. "Thank you," she breathed. Then she gathered her shorts and slipped out the door, leaving us in the sudden, charged silence.

I went to Jean, still kneeling on the bench. I tilted her chin up. "You were perfect," I whispered, then kissed her, tasting the stranger's tangy, musky release on her lips. It was fucking electric.

A small slot in the wall next to the door clicked open. Inside was another card and a single, ornate key.

Challenge accepted. Pleasure administered. Proceed to the next corridor. Use the key on the door marked with a V.

Jean stood on shaky legs, taking the key. Her eyes met mine, blazing with a fire that had only been stoked. The labyrinth had us. And we were only just beginning.

CHAPTER 13

Discovery Reshaped

The corridor beyond the door was narrow and silent, the only sound being our own rapid breaths. The ornate key felt heavy in Jean's hand. We moved, my palm on the small of her back, feeling the eager tension in her muscles. At the end of the hall, a single door bore a polished brass letter: V.

Jean slid the key into the lock. It turned with a satisfying, heavy *thunk*.

We pushed the door open together.

The scent hit us first—roasted meats, rich sauces, fresh bread. The room was a dining chamber, lit by crystal chandeliers, dominated by a long mahogany banquet table groaning under platters of food. Succulent roast fowl, glazed vegetables, towers of fruit, and decanters of deep red wine.

And standing at the head of the table, Ms. Adebayo.

She was a vision in head-to-toe black leather. A corset laced tightly over a sheer blouse, highlighting her magnificent tits. Leather pants hugged her powerful hips and thighs. Her dark espresso skin gleamed in the warm light.

"Welcome," she said, her voice a smooth, commanding purr. "You've passed the first gate. Now, you must refresh yourselves. *Eat. Drink*. You will need your strength." She gestured to the feast. "Take whatever you desire. I will be in the next room when you are ready."

She turned and disappeared through a curtained archway, the scent of her perfume lingering.

We didn't speak. We didn't need to. We filled our plates, the food exquisite, the wine dark and spicy. We ate with a strange, focused hunger, the silence between us thick with anticipation. My cock was already hard again, a persistent ache. I could see the flush on Jean's chest, the way her nipples pressed against the thin silk of her dress. We were fueling up for a different kind of feast.

When the last bite was swallowed, the last drop of wine drained, we rose as one and moved toward the curtain.

The next room was colder. Stone walls, dimmer light. Another long table, but this one was not set for dining.

It was an arsenal of pleasure and pain.

Paddles of polished wood and stingy leather lay beside floggers with falls of soft suede and brutal rubber. There were crops, canes, and a bewildering array of ropes and silken cords. Knives with blunt, decorative edges gleamed beside rows of dildos and vibrators in every size and grotesque shape. Plugs, beads, clamps, and things I didn't even have names for.

Ms. Adebayo stood in the center of the room, her arms crossed. "Your next choice," she announced. "Each of you will select three items from this table. Choose what speaks to you. Choose what you wish to give or what you wish to receive."

Jean moved first, her fingers trailing over the tools. She picked up a small, teardrop-shaped paddle with a velvet side and a smooth leather side. Next, a set of silver nipple clamps with delicate chains. Finally, she selected a thick, veined dildo, a deep purple, with a flared base.

My turn. My eyes scanned the table. I bypassed the knives and the heavier floggers. My hand closed around a long, flexible cane. I felt its weight. Next, a pair of heavy-duty leather cuffs. Last, I chose a broad, heavy paddle made of dark, polished walnut.

Ms. Adebayo nodded, a hint of a smile on her lips. "Good. Now, through there." She pointed to another archway. "And we will decide the roles."

The third room was circular, with a padded floor and a low, round platform in the center. The air was still, expectant. As we entered, two other people followed us in from a side door. A man and a woman, both around our age, dressed in simple gray linen pants and tops. They were attractive, with neutral, watchful expressions.

"These are our witnesses and participants," Ms. Adebayo said, moving to stand before us. She held up a single, gold coin. "The rules are simple. You will flip. Heads, you top. Tails, you bottom. The couple who wins the flip will wield the tools *you* chose against the losing couple. The strangers will assist, ensuring the scenes are... complete."

My throat went dry. Jean's hand found mine, squeezing tight. This was it. No watching from the sidelines. We were both in the arena now.

"Call it," Ms. Adebayo said to me, holding the coin on her thumb.

"Heads," I rasped.

The coin spun into the air, a flash of gold. It clattered onto the stone floor, spinning, then settled.

Tails.

A jolt went through me. *Bottom*. We were submitting.

Ms. Adebayo's smile widened. "Strip. Then assume your positions on the platform. On your knees, facing each other."

Our clothes fell away in a heap. The cool air raised goosebumps on our skin. Naked, we knelt on the padded dais, facing each other. Jean's eyes were huge, dark pools of fear and wild excitement. I reached out, cupping her face. "We're together," I whispered.

Ms. Adebayo handed our chosen tools to the strangers. The woman took Jean's paddle, clamps, and dildo. The man took my cane, cuffs, and the walnut paddle.

"Let us begin with binding," Ms. Adebayo commanded. "A foundation of restraint."

The male stranger moved behind me. He took the heavy leather cuffs and secured them tightly around my wrists. Then he pulled my arms behind my back, linking the cuffs together with a short chain. My shoulders pulled back, my chest thrust forward. I was immobilized.

The female stranger did the same to Jean, locking her wrists behind her. We were now kneeling, bound, utterly exposed to each other and to them.

"Now," Ms. Adebayo said, circling us like a panther. "A lesson in sensation." She nodded to the woman. "Start with her. The clamps."

The woman stepped in front of Jean. She held up the silver clamps, letting the chain dangle. She pinched Jean's right nipple, rolling it to a tight, pebbled peak. Jean gasped. Then the woman opened the clamp and fixed it onto the tender flesh.

"*Ah!*" Jean cried out, her back arching. The bite was sharp and immediate.

The woman repeated the process on her left nipple. Jean was panting now, the silver chains swaying between her tits, each small movement sending fresh jolts of pain through her.

"Good," Ms. Adebayo purred. "Now him. The cane."

The man moved behind me. I heard the soft *swish* of the cane through the air a split second before it landed.

THWACK!

A line of pure, fiery heat blossomed across my shoulders. I grunted, my muscles tensing.

THWACK!

Another stripe, lower this time, just above my ass. The pain was clean and bright, and it lit up my fucking nerve endings. My cock, trapped against my stomach, throbbed painfully.

"You may speak," Ms. Adebayo said. "You may beg, or you may encourage. Your choice."

Jean was looking at me, her eyes glazed. "Aaron..." she breathed.

"It's okay, baby," I gritted out as another stroke landed on my thighs. "Fuck, it's so... *sharp*."

The female stranger now picked up the teardrop paddle. She traced its velvet side over Jean's trembling stomach. "This side is for warmth," she said softly. Then she flipped it. "This side is for sting."

She drew back and smacked the leather side squarely across Jean's full, round ass cheek.

SMACK!

The sound was loud and crisp. Jean jerked against her bonds, a choked moan escaping her. A perfect, red imprint bloomed on her pale skin.

The man before me, still holding the cane, eyed the thick wooden paddle. "Your turn," he said, his voice bored, tentative. We were being used. We were being played. And we were _electric_, every nerve alive with sensation. Ms. Adebayo tapped the man on his shoulder, her voice smooth but commanding.

"I'll take over here," she said, her dark eyes glinting with intent. "I have something special in mind for Aaron."

The man stepped back without a word, handing her the cane. Ms. Adebayo circled me slowly, her leather pants creaking softly with each step. She stopped behind me, her presence radiating authority. Her fingers traced the reddened stripes on my back, sending shivers through me.

"You've taken the cane beautifully," she murmured, her voice low and intimate. "But I think it's time to... *elevate* the experience."

She struck again with the cane. It bit deep into the small space between my buttocks and the tops of my thighs. The burn was immediate. She slid the cane across my ass with deliberate slowness, the friction nearly unbearable. I gasped, my body trembling from the last stroke and the red welt it left. Ms. Adebayo set the cane aside and retrieved something from a nearby shelf—a slender, silver wand, its tip slightly curved and glinting in the dim light.

"This," she said, holding it up, "is for those who crave something more... *nuanced*."

She knelt behind me, her breath warm against my skin as she applied a generous amount of lube to the wand. The cool metal pressed against my sensitive entrance, and I tensed instinctively.

"Relax," she commanded, her tone leaving no room for resistance. "This will be *exquisite* if you let it."

With practiced precision, she pushed the wand inside me. It was shaped in a way that immediately brushed against something deep within me. My entire body jolted, a strangled moan escaping my lips.

"There it is," she purred, her voice dripping with satisfaction. She began to move the wand in slow, deliberate strokes, angling it to hit that spot with relentless accuracy.

The pleasure was sharp, almost too much, yet I couldn't help but rock back against her, craving more. My cock throbbed painfully, untouched and desperate. Jean's cries of ecstasy mingled with mine as we were both pushed to the edge by their relentless hands.

Ms. Adebayo leaned closer, her lips brushing my ear. "You're doing so well, Aaron," she whispered, her voice heavy with approval. "Now let's see how far we can take you."

The man was back, holding the heavy paddle in his hands. The paddle was a monster, and the man swinging it was brutal. It didn't sting. It *thudded.* A deep, resonant impact that drove the breath from my lungs when it connected with the meat of my ass. It wasn't just pain; it was a shockwave. My whole body rocked forward. A groan was torn from my throat.

"*Fuck yes*," I heard Jean whisper, staring at the reddening imprint on my skin. Five strokes was all I could stand. Sensing my limit being reached, Ms. Adebayo again tapped the man on his shoulder, her voice smooth as a command.

"I'll take it back over here," she said, her dark eyes glinting with intent. "I have something to ease the pain in mind for Aaron."

She moved behind me, her fingers deftly unbuckling the leather cuffs that held me in place. My arms fell to my sides, trembling from the strain and the anticipation of what was to come. She stood before me, her hands sliding down her own body as she peeled off the leather pants she wore, revealing long, toned legs and a perfect, round ass. She got down on her hands and knees, her back arched, her head turned to look at me over her shoulder.

"You will fuck me now, Aaron," she commanded, her voice dripping with authority. "Fuck me while he paddles your ass. You will not cum—not until I say you can."

Her words sent a shiver down my spine. I moved behind her, my cock throbbing painfully as I positioned myself at her entrance. She was already wet, her slickness glistening in the dim light. I pushed inside her in one smooth motion, groaning at the tight, warm embrace of her pussy.

As I began to thrust, the man behind me again picked up the paddle. The first stroke landed with a resounding *thud*, the impact reverberating through my body. I gritted my teeth, focusing on the rhythm of my hips as I buried myself deep inside Ms. Adebayo. Her moans mixed with the sound of the paddle striking my flesh, creating a symphony of pleasure and pain.

"Harder," she demanded, her voice breathless. "Fuck me harder, Aaron."

I obeyed, driving into her with increasing force. The paddle continued to fall, each stroke a sharp reminder of my submission. My entire world narrowed to the sensations—the heat of her pussy, the sting of the paddle, the new but overwhelming need to obey. I could feel the pressure building in my groin, but I held back, clinging to her command.

"Not yet," she purred, her voice a delicious torment. "You're doing so well, Aaron. Just a little longer."

We were trading blows now, a brutal symphony. SMACK! on Jean. THUD! It fell on me. Our breathing grew ragged and synchronized. The pain was morphing, melting into a thick, hot arousal that pooled in my gut. I could see the slickness glistening between Jean's spread thighs. The smell of her, of us, of sweat and leather and sex, filled the room.

The woman held up the thick purple dildo. "Jean," Ms. Adebayo commanded. "You will be filled. Aaron, you will be... drained."

The woman moved behind Jean. She pressed the blunt, silicone head against Jean's dripping cunt. Jean's eyes locked on mine, pleading, wanting. "Please," she whispered.

With one firm push, the woman buried the dildo inside her. Jean's head fell back, a long, guttural cry tearing from her throat. "*Oh GOD!*"

She was so fucking wet it slid in to the hilt in one smooth motion. The woman began to fuck her with it, a steady, deep rhythm that made Jean's whole body shake. The chains on her nipples jingled madly.

I was slamming into Ms. Adebayo in rhythm with the dildo invading Jean's wet pussy and the paddle relentlessly pounding my ass. The room was a cacophony of flesh meeting flesh, moans, and the sharp crack of wood and leather against skin. Jean's cries were growing more desperate, her body writhing as the dildo worked her deep, while I was lost in the tight, pulsing grip of Ms. Adebayo's cunt. Her back arched, her breath hitching as she reached her climax.

With a loud moan, Ms. Adebayo came, *squirting pulses of juice over my cock and balls.* Her pussy clenched around me like a vice, milking me relentlessly. "You may cum now, Aaron," she gasped, her voice thick with satisfaction. I didn't hold back. I thrust deep inside her one last time, my release surging through me as I emptied myself against her cervix.

I pulled my cock out, my cum mixing with her juices and spilling onto the polished wood floor. My legs trembled as I knelt there, spent and panting, the paddle finally still at my back. Jean's moans echoed through the room as the woman continued to fuck her with the dildo, her body jerking with each thrust.

Ms. Adebayo turned to face me, her chest heaving, a satisfied smile playing on her lips. "You did well," she said, her voice soft but commanding. She traced a finger along my jaw, wiping away a bead of sweat. "But we're not done yet."

The man stepped forward, his expression unreadable as he handed her a cloth to clean herself. Jean whimpered as the woman finally withdrew the dildo from her swollen cunt, leaving her trembling and empty.

"Stand," Ms. Adebayo commanded, and we obeyed, our bodies aching but somehow still craving more. The room was charged with energy, the air thick with the scent of sex and sweat. We stood before her, bare and vulnerable, waiting for her next move.

"You've both been so good," she purred, her eyes glinting with mischief. "But now, it's time for the final act."

CHAPTER 14

Discovery on Display

Ms. Adebayo led us through another door, leaving the damp, musky room behind. We didn't bother with clothes. We walked naked down a short, plush hallway, our bare feet sinking into the carpet. My ass throbbed with a deep, satisfying ache, and Jean's tits swayed, the silver clamps still dangling from her nipples, the chains clicking softly with each step. We were raw, open, and buzzing.

The door at the end opened silently.

The room was large, circular, and softly lit by sconces on the walls. A low, padded bench sat in the exact center under a single, focused spotlight. Around the perimeter, maybe a dozen people milled about, their voices a low, civilized murmur.

The men were all in dark coats and ties. Elegant. The women were draped in gorgeous gowns—silks, satins, and velvets—in deep jewel tones. Every dress seemed designed to showcase slits up to the hip, plunging necklines that revealed soft, powdered cleavage, and backs cut down to the curve of the ass. They held delicate crystal glasses. They were beautiful and refined.

And we were naked.

All conversation stopped as we entered. A dozen pairs of eyes turned to us. Not with shock, but with a calm, appraising interest. A collector's gaze.

"This is the viewing room," Ms. Adebayo said, her voice carrying in the quiet space. She placed a hand on Jean's lower back and gave her a gentle push forward. "Jean, the center is yours. Aaron, you will observe from here with me."

Jean's breath hitched, but her chin went up. She walked, fully nude, through the crowd. They parted for her, their eyes tracing the curves of her body, the red marks on her ass, and the glint of the clamps. She reached the bench and stood beside it, waiting.

A man in a perfectly tailored tuxedo stepped forward first. He was older, with silver hair and an air of quiet authority. He didn't speak. He simply reached out and took one of Jean's breasts in his hand, his thumb brushing over the clamped nipple. Jean gasped, her eyes fluttering closed for a second.

"Exquisite texture," the man remarked to no one in particular, his voice cultured. He squeezed gently, then moved his hand down her side, over the swell of her hip. He traced the line of one of the paddle marks. "Responsive canvas, but I see she has no tattoos yet."

Another woman, stunning in an emerald green gown, approached. Her fingers, cool and smooth, trailed up Jean's inner thigh. "May I?" she asked, her voice a whisper.

Jean nodded, biting her lip. "Yes."

The woman's fingers found Jean's cunt, which was already glistening, swollen from the dildo and the arousal of being watched. She parted Jean's lips with two fingers, exposing her pink, slick inner flesh to the light. "Beautifully engorged," the woman noted clinically, but her own breath quickened. She pressed a finger inside, just to the first knuckle, and Jean's knees buckled slightly. "And very, very wet."

I stood beside Ms. Adebayo, my cock hardening again as I watched. This was different. This was cold, clinical worship. It was fucking electric.

Another man, younger, with a hawk-like intensity, moved in. He prodded at Jean's asshole with a blunt, lubricated finger. "Tight," he announced. "But pliable. The previous play has made her receptive." He pushed in, and Jean cried out, a sharp, wanton sound that echoed in the hushed room. He worked his finger in and out slowly, his other hand gripping her hip. "She's taking it beautifully."

They were treating her like a prized animal at auction. Probing, inspecting, commenting on her worth. And Jean was *melting*. Her head was lolling back, her chest heaving. The humiliation, the exposure, and the sheer *attention* were fucking narcotic to her.

The main door opened again.

A young man walked in. He couldn't have been more than twenty-five. He was dressed simply in black trousers and a white shirt, sleeves rolled up. He had the lean, defined build of an athlete, a dusting of dark hair on his chest, and a confident, hungry look in his eye. His cock was already a thick, impressive outline against his pants.

Ms. Adebayo leaned into me. "His name is Lucas. He is on staff here. You might remember him. He brought your drinks to the gazebo the other night. He has... earned a participation token."

Lucas's eyes locked on Jean. He walked straight through the crowd, who now formed a loose circle around the bench. He stopped in front of her. He didn't touch her. He just looked, his gaze traveling from her flushed face, down her trembling body, to her glistening cunt.

My voice, when it came, was rough but clear. "Jean."

Her eyes, hazy with lust, snapped to mine across the room.

"Start with your mouth," I commanded. "Get on your knees and suck his cock. Show everyone how good you are at that. Show them how fucking hungry you are for it."

A shudder ran through her. She dropped to her knees on the padded floor before Lucas, her hands coming to rest on his thighs. Her tits hung heavy, the clamps swaying. Lucas undid his fly, and his cock sprang out. It was perfect—long, thick, veined, already dripping a bead of pre-cum from the slit.

Jean didn't hesitate. She leaned forward, her tongue darting out to catch that drop. She swallowed it with a soft moan. Then she opened her mouth wide and took the head of his cock inside.

The room was utterly silent except for the wet, sucking sounds.

She took him deep, her nose pressing into his trimmed pubic hair. Her head began to bob, a slow, deep rhythm. Her lips stretched taut around his girth. One of her hands came up to cradle his balls, rolling them gently. The other stroked the base of his shaft.

"*Fuck*, that's good," Lucas breathed, his hands tangling in her curly hair. He didn't force her. He just held on, his hips giving tiny, involuntary thrusts.

I could see everything. The way her cheeks hollowed. The shine of her saliva coating his length. The desperate, worshipful look in her eyes as she gazed up at him. The guests pressed closer, their own arousal palpable. A woman in a red dress had her hand subtly between her own thighs, rubbing through the silk.

Jean picked up the pace, slurping, gagging gently, and then pulling back to swirl her tongue around the head. She was fucking *performing*. For me. For them. For him.

"She's a natural cocksucker," the silver-haired man observed quietly to his companion.

"I want to see her face when he comes," the woman in green replied, her voice husky.

Lucas's control broke. His thighs tensed. "Gonna cum," he grunted. "Gonna fill your fucking throat."

Jean pulled off with a lewd *pop*. "Do it," she panted, her lips swollen. "Give it to me. I want to taste it."

He didn't need telling twice. He gripped his cock and stroked it furiously. With a sharp cry, he erupted. Thick, white ropes of cum shot across Jean's face. The first landed on her cheek. The second streaked across her lips and chin. The third splattered on her collarbone. She stuck her tongue out, catching what she could, swallowing greedily, then licking her lips clean.

The guests murmured in appreciation.

Before she could recover, Lucas hauled her to her feet and turned her around, bending her over the padded bench. Her ass was in the air, her cunt and asshole on full display, dripping with her own juices. He spat into his hand, slicked his cock with his saliva and his own sperm, and positioned himself at her entrance.

He looked at me, a question in his eyes. I gave a single, firm nod.

He slammed into her.

Jean screamed, a raw, joyous sound of pure penetration. He fucked her hard and deep, his balls slapping against her wet folds. The bench creaked with the force. The guests closed the circle completely now, their faces inches from the action. They watched, mesmerized, as his cock pistoned in and out of her stretched, glistening hole.

"Look at her take it," a man whispered, adjusting his own straining trousers.

"So deep," a woman breathed, her hand now openly cupping her breast.

Lucas pulled out, his cock gleaming. "Other side," he growled. He pushed her legs together, turning her onto her back on the bench. He climbed on top, driving into her in a missionary position, but brutal, her legs hooked over his shoulders. This angle was deeper. Jean's eyes rolled back. "Oh god, oh god... right *there*!"

He was hammering her cervix. She was so wet, the sound was a filthy, rhythmic squelch. He leaned down, capturing her mouth in a rough, cum-flavored kiss.

I was so hard, it hurt. Ms. Adebayo's hand rested on my arm, her nails digging in slightly. "She is everything we hoped for," she murmured.

Lucas changed again, pulling out and spinning her onto her hands and knees. "Doggy," he commanded. He mounted her from behind again, but this time, one hand snaked around to her clit, rubbing rough circles. The other gripped her hip, his fingers leaving bruises.

Jean was babbling. "Yes! Fuck me! Don't stop! I'm going to cum... I'm going to cum on your fucking cock!"

The guests were no longer quiet. There were soft moans and the rustle of fabric as hands wandered. They were getting off on this.

On watching his thick, veiny tool disappear into her used, willing cunt, over and over.

Lucas's pace became frantic, punishing. "Gonna breed this cunt!" he snarled, his orgasm building.

"Do it!" I shouted from the sidelines, my own hand moving to my cock, stroking in time with his thrusts. "Fill her up, Lucas!"

With a final, brutal drive, he buried himself to the hilt and roared. His body convulsed as he pumped his second load deep into Jean's pussy. She screamed, her own orgasm ripping through her, her cunt milking him, her juices mixing with his cum and leaking out around his still-throbbing cock.

He collapsed on top of her for a moment, both of them panting. Then he pulled out slowly.

A rivulet of white immediately began to trickle out of Jean's well-fucked hole, down her inner thigh, onto the dark leather of the bench.

The guests exhaled a collective, shuddering breath. The show wasn't over. I could see it in their eyes. They wanted more. Another man, older, with a stern face, was already loosening his tie, his gaze fixed on Jean's spent, dripping body. He stepped forward, his voice a low rumble in the charged silence.

CHAPTER 15

Discovery Rewarded

The heavy door to the viewing room closed behind us, sealing off the murmur of the guests. Ms. Adebayo stood before us, still fully dressed, her expression unreadable as she looked at our naked, sweat-slicked, and cum-stained bodies.

"Come with me," she said, her voice softer now.

We followed a silent, ragged procession through a final, unmarked door. It didn't lead to another Labyrinth chamber. It opened into a quiet, carpeted office. A large mahogany desk. Bookshelves. Soft lamplight. It felt jarringly normal.

She walked behind her desk and sat. She gestured to the two plush chairs opposite her. "Please."

We sat, suddenly aware of our nudity in this formal space. Jean's cunt was still dripping Lucas's cum onto the expensive leather seat.

Ms. Adebayo folded her hands. "The labyrinth is complete. You have navigated every chamber and met every challenge I set before you." A small, genuine smile touched her lips. "You have exceeded every expectation."

She opened a drawer and produced a simple, heavy keycard. She slid it across the desk toward me. "This is a master key. Your original suite is yours for three more nights, completely complimentary. Room service, the restaurants, the bars—all of it is on the house. The facilities... the pool, the gym, the *private* lounges... are all open to you."

She leaned back, her dark eyes moving from me to Jean. "You may interact with other guests, should you wish. Or you may spend your time entirely together. The choice is now, and entirely, yours."

The finality of it was a physical release. The pressure, the orchestrated madness, just... evaporated. I looked at Jean. Her face was a mess—smudged mascara and dried streaks of Lucas's cum on her cheek. She looked utterly wrecked. And more beautiful than I had ever seen her.

"Thank you," I managed to say, my voice hoarse.

Ms. Adebayo merely nodded. "Enjoy your stay."

We stood, clutching the keycard, and left the office. A short, private elevator whisked us directly to our floor. The silence between us was thick, but it wasn't awkward. It was saturated. *Full.*

The door to our suite clicked open. The familiar space, untouched since this morning, felt like a sanctuary. I closed the door, locked it, and leaned back against it.

Jean stood in the center of the living room, her back to me. Her shoulders were trembling.

I crossed the space in two strides and turned her to face me. I cupped her filthy, beautiful face in my hands.

"Jean," I whispered, my throat tight. "My god, Jean."

Her eyes, wide and deep, searched mine.

The words poured out of me, raw and unfiltered. "I love you. I love you so fucking much it feels like my heart is going to explode. I love being with you. I love watching you. I love *sharing with* you. I love the fucking fire in you. I love that you are *mine* and you are *everyone's* and you are so fucking *alive*."

A sob hitched in her chest, but she was smiling. A tear cut through the mess on her cheek. "Aaron..."

"No one else tonight," I said, my voice dropping to a growl. "No one to watch. No one to share. No one to participate. Just me. Just you. Just *us*."

I crashed my lips onto hers. The kiss wasn't gentle. It was a claiming. A homecoming. I could taste the salt of her tears, the faint, bitter remnant of another man's release. I licked it clean, my tongue sweeping into her mouth, and she moaned, her hands clawing at my back.

I broke the kiss and started walking her backward toward the bedroom. With every step, I tore at the remnants of our night. I wiped the cum from her face with my thumbs, then licked them clean, staring into her eyes. "Mine," I growled.

We fell onto the bed, a tangle of limbs. For a long moment, we just kissed, deeply, slowly, relearning the map of each other's mouths. My hands roamed her body—over the fading paddle marks on her ass, the sensitive skin around the clamp-bruised nipples, and the slick heat between her legs.

"You're so wet," I murmured against her neck, sucking the skin there. "Is this all for me now? This dripping, messy, *perfect* cunt? Is this all mine?"

"Yes," she gasped, arching her back. "*Yes*, Aaron. It's yours. It's always been yours. It's just been... waiting for you to come home to it."

I moved down her body. I kissed every bruise, every mark. I took one tender, swollen nipple into my mouth, sucking gently, and she cried out, her fingers threading through my hair. I kissed my way down her stomach, through the thatch of curls, and buried my face between her thighs.

Her scent was a complex, intoxicating mix—her own sweet arousal, the musk of sex, the lingering, salty tang of Lucas's cum. I didn't care. I lapped at it all. I pressed my tongue flat against her slit and licked upward, gathering the combined flavors of our adventure. I pushed my tongue inside her, fucking her with it, curling it to reach that spot that made her scream.

"Oh, *fuck*! Right there! *Don't stop!*" Her hips bucked off the bed.

I fucked her with my tongue, deep and slow, then fast and shallow. I focused on her clit, circling it with the very tip, then sucking it hard between my lips. Her legs shook. Her moans became a continuous, desperate song.

"I'm gonna... Aaron, I'm going to cum from just your mouth... please..."

I slid two fingers inside her soaked, tight channel, crooking them to press against that spongy front wall. I sucked her clit and fucked her with my fingers, and I felt her cunt clench, a fluttering, violent pulse.

She came with a shattered cry, her back bowing off the mattress. Her juices flooded my mouth, hot and sweet. I drank her down, fucking her through the quakes until she was limp and panting.

I crawled up her body, my cock—aching, neglected, *desperate*—slapping against her stomach. I positioned myself at her entrance. I looked into her hazy, sated eyes.

"Look at me," I commanded, my voice rough with need. "I want you to see me when I fill you up. I want you to know it's *me*."

She nodded, her gaze locking onto mine. "I see you. I *need* you."

I pushed inside.

It was different. *So* different. There was no audience. No performance. Just the two of us, and the slow, inexorable slide of my cock into her impossibly hot, impossibly tight, *familiar* cunt. She was so open, so relaxed from her orgasm and the night's activities, yet she gripped me like a velvet fist.

"*God... Jean...*" I sank to the hilt, my balls pressing against her ass. The feeling was overwhelming. Possessive. Primal.

I began to move. Slow, deep, grinding strokes. Each thrust dragged against her inner walls, each withdrawal made her gasp. I leaned down, bracing my arms on either side of her head, our faces inches apart. Our breath mingled.

"This is what it's for," I whispered, driving into her again. "All of it. The watching. The sharing. It all comes back to this. To me, being inside you. To you reminding me why I fucking *live* to see you on your knees for another man."

"Yes," she breathed, her eyes glazing with a new kind of pleasure. "It makes this... *more*."

"It makes you *more*," I corrected, my pace increasing. The bed began to rock. The headboard tapped the wall in a steady, driving rhythm. "It makes you the most vibrant, alive, *fucking* perfect woman on the planet."

I hooked my arms under her knees, pushing them back toward her shoulders. The angle changed, and I hit a depth that made her eyes fly wide open. "*Aaron!*"

"Say it," I grunted, pistoning into that spot, over and over. "Who's fucking you?"

"You are!" she screamed.

"Who owns this cunt?"

"You do! You *own* it!"

"And who do you love?" I was slamming into her now, my control fraying. The sounds were obscene: skin on skin, the wet slap of our bodies, her ragged cries.

"You! I love *you*!"

Her second orgasm tore through her, a silent, breathless wave that made her cunt spasm and clutch at my cock in rhythmic, milking pulls. It was too much. The visual of her face, the feel of her squeezing me, the emotional fucking *flood* of the entire night...

My climax erupted from my balls like a dam breaking. I drove in as deep as I could, my body locking, and I came. I came harder than I ever had in my life. Thick, hot pulses of cum shot deep into her womb, a claiming, a sealing. I shouted her name, a raw, broken sound, as I emptied myself into her, filling her with *my* seed, marking her as *mine* in the most basic way.

I collapsed on top of her, spent, my heart hammering against her chest. We lay there, a tangled, sweaty, sticky mess, our breathing slowly syncing.

After a long while, I rolled to the side, pulling her with me, keeping myself buried inside her. I didn't want to leave her warmth.

She nuzzled into my neck, her lips brushing my skin. "I love you," she whispered, her voice thick with sleep and satisfaction.

I held her tighter. The labyrinth was behind us. For the next three nights, the world was ours. And as I felt her relax completely into sleep, her cunt still gently pulsing around my softening cock, I knew exactly what I wanted to do.

www.ingramcontent.com/pod-product-compliance
Lightning Source LLC
LaVergne TN
LVHW010923110826
845149LV00013B/2465

* 9 7 8 1 9 7 2 7 1 0 5 2 4 *